Eleanor —
Happy reading and
happy sewing!
Kathryn R. Biel

Made for Me

By

Kathryn R. Biel

MADE FOR ME

ISBN-10: 0-9971939-3-X
ISBN-13: 978-0-9971939-3-0

This book is a work of fiction. Names, characters, places, and incidents are either products of the author's imagination or are used fictitiously and any resemblance to actual persons, living or dead, business establishments, events or locales is purely coincidental.

Cover design by Becky Monson.
Cover image via depositphotos.com by lianella.

Dedication

To Michele, obviously:

Now you've got a whole book about you, except it's not about you at all. I can't thank you enough for being my person through all of this and so much more.

Chapter 1

Ugh. I'm so full. I've never been this full. Well, not since last Christmas Eve. I do this to myself every year. My mom and Aunt Rosalie go to town, and I lose all self-control.

What little self-control I possess, which isn't much.

I ate all seven fishes this year. Usually I only make it to five fishes, but this year I went for the whole enchilada. Or pesce, as the case may be. Shrimp cocktail, lox, smelts, and crab dip. Scallops, baccala, and salmon. Not to mention the broccoli rabe and then the desserts. I'm a sucker for those little Italian cookies.

Now I think my stomach is going to explode. Or at least the button on my pants is. I reach my hand oh so discreetly under my sweater and release the button. Aaaaaah, sweet relief.

I'd had the cutest little shift dress to wear, until Mom decided that we needed to make this an ugly Christmas sweater party. I wouldn't have felt so constricted in my dress. I don't wear these kinds of clothes often—conservative pants and a sweater. If Barrett had been with me, I would not have been caught dead in this. Totally not my style. My mom, on the other hand, is the queen of the turtleneck and sweater. Gives me hives really.

Or maybe that's the shellfish.

Either way, you can stick a fork in me. I'm done.

I look at my watch. It's only seven p.m. Oh good Lord. Only five more hours until Midnight Mass. I either need a nap or a roll of Tums. Maybe both. I sneak down the hall to my old bedroom. I've got to get out of these terrible clothes. Maybe I can take a quick nap, sleep off the wine, and then drive home and change before Mass. I should have brought a change of clothes with me.

Don't get me wrong—I love my family. I love having aunts and uncles and cousins. My brothers, sister, and I add to the melee. We're all loud and noisy. The laughs flow as freely as the wine does. That's when we're all speaking to each other. Which is almost never. But that's not why I ate my weight in seafood tonight.

Oh, no, I strapped on the feedbag so I wouldn't have to answer questions about why I'm single. Again. Every time a well-meaning cousin or nosy aunt asked a question, I shoved a forkful of fish into my mouth. My sister is a no-show this year and my brothers are both with their wives' families. So the target seems to be firmly planted on me this year. Like it's a crime to be almost thirty and still unmarried. Just because no female in our family has dared remain single this long doesn't make it a crime.

I can't believe Barrett ditched me on Christmas Eve. This is not the first time this has happened. I'd like to say it will be the last, but I'm not hopeful.

Barrett and I have one of those super-complex, on-again-off-again relationships. When we're together, the chemistry is unbelievable. And then it's not.

We're in a not phase right now.

Which is fine, because I know we'll be back together soon. I'm totally okay taking a break.

It's just ... well, I told my mom he was coming.

She told Aunt Rosalie. Who told Aunt Maria. Who told my cousins Antonia, Alessandra, Carmalina, and Tony. I'm fairly certain my uncles Mario and Vito know as well, but I don't think they give a hoot.

Sometimes I feel naming the members of my family tree is like reciting the cast list from *The Sopranos*. Which is why I don't fit in. My name is Michele. It's not even remotely Italian. And to make matters worse, I'm blond.

Well, I used to be.

I maintain that I still am. That secret is safe with my hairdresser. I was blond as a child. Pale skin, blue eyes. Yeah, clichéd I know. It's not my fault. Blame my Polish father. My mom is only half-Italian to begin with. Her own mother strayed with a Scotsman.

At least I'm short like the rest of my Italian family members. I fit right in there. 5'1". That's it. I kind of like hanging with my cousins. Carmalina is the tallest female at 5'4", and the men don't get much taller than about 5'8". It's a sharp contrast to my best friend, Christine, who hovers around Jolly Green Giant height.

My family can be kind of ... intense. They are noisy and boisterous and get all up in everyone's business. I may have been complaining about this to Barrett. I wonder if that has anything to do with his breaking things off last week. I mean, who dumps someone the week before Christmas?

Barrett Synder, that's who.

Maybe he was scared to meet my family. I guess we can be a bit on the overwhelming side. That's probably what it is.

"Michele, are you in there?"

Drat. My mom has found me.

"Yeah, I'll be right out."

That doesn't stop my mom from coming in. Oh right, no privacy. That's why I'm not planning on staying here tonight. "What are you doing in here?"

"Just sleeping off dinner."

"People are asking about you. You need to come out and join us for coffee. I need your help cleaning up."

Ooops, I forgot I told Mom I'd help her. With my sister Lynn on vacation with her husband, she needs the extra hand. They're trying to get pregnant and wanted a romantic baby-making holiday. Good for them. Lynn's thirty-seven, and that biological clock is ticking so loudly even I can hear it. They sort of thought the stress of the holidays wouldn't help, so they decided to skip it this year. Though I don't envy the heartbreak they've undergone, I'm sort of jealous that they get to be absent from all this fun. My mom is recovering from chemo and radiation, and her stamina is not what it once was. "Sorry!" I jump up off the bed and shimmy around trying to button my pants. "I was in a little bit of a food coma."

"I'm ready for a nap myself."

"Why don't you go lie down, and I'll take care of the kitchen?"

"I can't do that. I'm the hostess."

I look at her, and see fatigue hanging heavily around her eyes and mouth. I can't believe I was so selfish as to hole myself up in here. To let myself wallow about Barrett. Stupid Barrett. I should be happy for my family. We've been through a lot this year.

"You rest. I'll take over hostess duties. And it's not like it's company. It's just family."

"I guess. You'll have to figure out how to do this. I won't always be here, you know."

In light of the current situation, her words should make my heart ache. But here's the thing—my mom is queen of the guilt trip. We've been hearing about her imminent demise my whole life. I wish Lynn were here. We'd be rolling our eyes. We've made drinking games out of it in the past. Last year, we were almost passed-out drunk before Mass.

Of course, then doesn't she go and get diagnosed with breast cancer in April. Maybe she made all those comments because deep down she knew she was sick, but I think it's more likely her guilt-inducing tendencies were simply those of many a good Italian-Catholic mother. After all, guilt is the cornerstone of her manipulation. I mean power.

It was all a trap. I mean, I have no doubt my mom's a little—lot—tired. She's been cooking for days. Not to mention hitting the cab pretty hard. But that's not what this is all about. Oh no.

Aunt Maria pounces before I get the first dish packaged up. The men folk "helped out" by piling up all the platters of food on the kitchen counter in order to make room for the desserts. Now, it's up to me to portion out take-home containers and put away the leftovers.

"So, I hear that you're looking for a man."

My teeth clench when I realize the trap I've walked into. "Um, no, not really. I'm involved with someone."

"That's not what I hear. I hear he broke up with you again. I mean, who breaks up with someone the week before Christmas?"

Would it be wrong of me to fake appendicitis?

"We're just taking a little bit of a break. We're not at the point where we're ready to meet each other's families."

"Are you sleeping together?"

"I ... um ... Aunt Maria! That's personal." I'm sure my face is as red as the Santa's sequined hat adorning my sweater.

"If you're committed enough for hanky panky, then he should be man enough to meet your family."

Sheesh, she's so old fashioned.

Although, she may have a point. She continues her yammering, but now my thoughts are drifting toward Barrett. We're good in the bedroom department, if you know what I mean, but every time I mention something serious, Barrett seems to pull back. Within a few days, he breaks it off. Then, a few weeks later, he'll call again—usually late at night—and wham!—we're back together.

Huh. Now that I think about it, maybe it's not the best situation. Aunt Maria has continued talking, but I've managed to tune her out. But a few words get through and sound the alarm bells.

"Wait—what was that?"

"I said, you've messed your life up enough with that dead-end job and loser boyfriends. I'm taking over. Little Joey Frangella will be here any minute to meet you. You're going to go out on five dates with him. I promised his mother."

"Aunt Maria! You can't do that!"

"Yes I can. Your mother isn't up to it right now. She could die you know. And you're not getting any younger. Your eggs will be all dried up and won't hatch, if you know what I mean. You don't want to end up like your sister, waiting too long, if you know what I mean. Although with the way you run around, I'm surprised you haven't gotten yourself into a *situation*, if you know what I mean." She elbows me. She's well known for saying 'if you know what I mean' after every sentence. I don't even hear it anymore. Because, of course, I know what she means. She's not subtle. I also know how to take my birth control pill every morning. I don't share that with her though.

The doorbell rings. Aunt Maria puts down the dish towel she's been using to dry dishes. "Oh, that's Little Joey right now!"

The thing with Italians—there are only about five names they ever use. So, undoubtedly, Little Joey's father is Big Joey (and his grandfather is Papa Joey). It may not be a comment on his stature or size of ... other things (shudder). I hope.

I think about climbing out the window, but I know there's nowhere to hide.

"Mmm, mmm, mmm. If you're this good looking from the back, I can't wait to see you from the front."

This does not bode well. Not well at all.

Chapter 2

I don't want to be unkind, especially not on the eve of our Lord's birth, but ick. Gack. Blech.

That's how I'd describe Little Joey. First of all, let's disperse with the "Little." Joey is about 6'3" and probably about 350 pounds. He's super tall, so the weight isn't bad. It's just ... well, he's a hulking beast of a man. I think he spends a lot of time at the gym, as his biceps are about the size of my waist. How do I know this? Despite the fact that it's December in Upstate New York, Joey is wearing a skin-tight T-shirt. And gold chains. As in multiple.

I think he skips the ab workout, not that I blame him, but his gut is round and emphasized by his toddler-sized shirt. Of course, I'm wearing an ugly Christmas sweater and khakis, so I can't judge. Well, I shouldn't judge, but I do.

Now, the Italian Stallion thing may be some women's ideal, but it's not mine. While I like being part Italian myself, it's not a requirement for me in a potential mate. I'm not one of those Italians who only dates other Italians. And Joey oozes Italian-ness out of every pore. Well, he's oozing something. He really needs to let up on the hair grease.

But physique and excess hair product aside are not my biggest problems with Little Joey Frangella. My main issue is that after coming in and ogling my back side, he proceeds to pick me up and lift me overhead, like he's bench pressing me.

"Look at this! I could probably bench two of you!"

I don't take being manhandled well, and I fight to get down. Apparently Joey isn't used to a bar that moves, and he drops me. Right on my rear, right in the middle of a kitchen full of people.

Forget five; I'm not going out on one single date with him.

The fiasco in the kitchen has created quite the stir, and I look up to see that not only Aunt Maria and Uncle Mario, but all of my cousins, have witnessed the spectacle. In addition, Tony's best friend, Lincoln, crowds in, followed by my mom and my brother, John, who's just shown up. At least his wife, with whom I'm not terribly close (okay, I sort of hate her) isn't here to witness my plummet.

And you know, when they say things can't get any worse, they somehow seem to? Yeah, I split my pants. Right up the back seam.

Please kill me now.

My butt is aching, and there's a breeze where it shouldn't be. The howls of laughter fill the kitchen, and I can feel my face on fire.

Carmalina pulls me to my feet. John laughed so hard that his asthma kicked in, and now he's coughing up a lung. Serves him right.

The big lunk head—aka Little Joey—is just standing there. His mouth is open. I can't even. I so can't even. I want to storm out of the room, but the breeze on my butt precludes me from marching out with any sort of dignity. So glad I'm wearing a thong today. Instead, I inch backwards, pressing my behind into the sink cabinet and glare. I've got a pretty good glare, and the lunk head gets the memo.

"Ooops, sorry."

"Sorry? That's all you've got to say? Sorry?" My voice may have a super attractive squeaky quality.

"You shouldn't of moved so much. It's like you got ants in your pants or somethin'. I bet you're a mess."

The kitchen is a flurry of activity, and I want to fall through the floor. My cousin Antonia hands me a glass of red, which I promptly drain in one swift motion. Setting the glass on the counter, it is immediately snatched up by Aunt Rosalie who attempts to wash it. It's a little difficult, considering I'm still glued to the front of the sink. It doesn't seem to matter to her, as she delivers a few jabby elbows to my back. At least the glass is clean. That's all that matters.

Little Joey has gone in search of some food. The next round of pastries and cookies is coming out. John, done for the moment laughing at me, drifts out to the living room to visit with Dad and the uncles. Carm and Antonia are still buzzing around, making sure I'm okay. It's getting annoying.

"Yes, yes, I'm fine." My butt hurts, but no way I'm telling them that. The issue of the sudden ventilation in the back of my pants is more of a concern. "I've got to go home and change." In the back of my head, I'm sort of contemplating ditching Mass and just going to bed. But I know my mom would never forgive me, especially this year. Grabbing a soggy dish towel, I cover my backside and leave the safety of the cabinets.

"Wait, where are you going?" Aunt Maria—who started all this in the first place by setting me up with Little Joey—steps in front of me.

"I have to go home and change. My pants are split."

"You can't drive. You just had a glass of wine. I saw you." Aunt Maria is sort of a fanatic about that. Ever since Uncle Vito got a DWI two years ago, she's taken it upon herself to closely monitor everyone's drinking and driving. I'm surprised she'll let Uncle Vito drive after taking the communion wine.

"I'm fine. It was only a glass." Never mind that I shotgunned it. "I have to go home. My pants are totally split up the back. I can't go to Christmas Mass with my bum hanging out."

Aunt Maria quickly blesses herself. "No, that won't work, if you know what I mean." Then, in a loud voice, much louder than one would expect out of a short little lady, she bellows, "WHO HERE HASN'T HAD A DRINK IN THE PAST HOUR?"

I glance out into the living room. My dad is asleep in his recliner. I guess it doesn't matter that there's a house full of people. John has a highball glass in his hand, and he's doing his best to drain it. Bottles of beer and wine glasses cover almost every flat surface in the room. Carm and Antonia are pink-faced and sloppy. They've put away at least a bottle each. Aunt Rosalie doesn't drive, and my mom's still resting. And there is no way on God's green earth that I'm going anywhere with Little Joey.

"I'm fine." Lincoln comes into the kitchen. Lincoln's one of those additional family members. He lives next door to Tony, which is how they became fast friends. The inseparable kind. I'm not sure that I've ever seen one without the other. Lincoln is right smack dab in the middle of six sisters, so I think the solitude and testosterone next door was a welcome change. "I haven't been drinking. I can drive you home."

"Thanks. I'm fine, but ..."

"But I know how Mama Maria is."

Truth. There's no arguing with her.

"Thanks. I appreciate it. Let me just get my coat and stuff."

"Sure. Why don't we take your car, and then you can bring me back to church? I can go home with Tony from there."

I look at my watch. It's only 9:30. Gosh, how is it only 9:30? Of course, we have to get to the church a little after 11 to get a seat, so that's not bad. Maybe Lincoln won't mind if I take a quick catnap at home.

Once in the car, exhaustion takes over. "You know, I think I'm more tired than anything else."

"Well, sleepy driving is no less dangerous than drunk driving."

"No, I know. Thanks for giving me a lift. I've been trying to figure out a way to get out of there for hours. I guess I should have thought about getting tossed around and dropped like a sack of potatoes earlier."

"Yeah, what was that?"

"Aunt Maria is—was—trying to set me up with Little Joey. Like that's ever going to happen."

"Why would she do that?"

I can't contain the sigh. "Because I'm not married. Because I'm not dating. Well, sort of. Not really, but kind of."

"What does that even mean?"

"My Facebook status is 'It's complicated.'"

"It's not that complicated. Either you are dating someone or you're not."

"We're currently off again, but I have no reason to think that soon we won't be on again."

"Why?"

"Why what? Why are we off again, or why do I think we'll be back on again soon?"

Lincoln laughs. "Yes to both. I don't understand the on-again, off-again thing."

I look over at him, his face illuminated by the lights of the dashboard. His jaw has filled out nicely and is perfectly square from the side. It's almost as if he's becoming a man. When did that happen?

"It's just that Barrett and I are very compatible in some ways, and not so much in others. We're trying to figure it out. Honestly, I think he's intimidated by meeting my family and didn't want to do it."

"You know, your family is part of you. If someone doesn't want to meet them, that's a big red flag."

"Now you sound like Aunt Maria."

"Too many years spent in her kitchen, I guess, if you know what I mean." He puts the emphasis on her catch phrase. I can see that he's smiling, and has dimples.

"Nice. I do know what you mean. Now, enough about me. Tell me about you. How's school going? Where are you again?"

"I got my MBA from Cornell two years ago. I've been working for a broadcasting company. I started basically as an administrative assistant but was recently promoted to assistant strategy design manager."

"Wait, aren't you twelve? How are you out in the real world?" Tony and Lincoln are younger than I am. They were always buzzing around, doing little boy stuff, making little-boy messes.

"My boyish good looks may scream youth, but I'm a wise old man under this exterior."

"You'll always be a little boy to me."

"And you'll always be an old lady to me." He laughs.

I whack him lightly on the arm. "Thanks a lot for that."

"What about you? What are you doing now? Is it still fashion?"

Inwardly I sigh. Okay, I sigh outwardly too. I hate these questions. "I'm still working at U'nique Boutique. It's a job."

"Weren't you going to become a famous fashion designer?"

We're pulling up to my apartment, which spares me from having to come up with an answer. My coat thankfully covers my back end as I slide out of the car. I guess my desire to get out of this heinous sweater will be fulfilled. The only desire of mine tonight. My apartment's on the second floor. Lincoln follows me up. I hope he can't see my butt.

"Make yourself comfortable. Help yourself to anything in the kitchen. I'll be out in a few."

18

Once I disrobe, I hesitate about what to do with my torn pants. I should fix them—I certainly have the ability. Years of sewing and even some design classes ensure that. I never want to wear them again. I'll forever think about this night.

The night when I had to show up (yet again) unmarried and unattached. When my mom had to rest to make it through the evening. When my aunts thought I was so pitiful that they set me up with a beast who tossed me around like I meant nothing. When I find out the pesky kid who is my little cousin's age not only has an Ivy League MBA but an actual job where he's moving up the ranks.

And then there's me. In a dead-end job, wasting my talent. Wasting my life. Throwing the pants out would be a waste, but that's just how I feel—a waste.

Chapter 3

"Hey, Christine, it's me. Just checking in to see what you're up to today. Last night was insane, and not in a good crazy way. I ... I can't even. Why don't you come with me to dinner at my folks' and I'll fill you in? Call me."

"Hey, Lynn. Merry Christmas! Oh my God, you are never leaving me alone with the family like that again. My butt will never be the same. Hope you're having fun. Love you!"

It's eleven a.m., and I've already struck out twice. Do I dare go for a third?

Of course I do, because I'm an imbecile.

"Hey, Barrett. It's me. I just wanted to wish you a Merry Christmas. Hope you're having a nice holiday. Give me a call if you get a chance. Or not. Whatever. It's cool. Okay, I've—I'm gonna go. Hope to talk soon. Or not. Gah! Bye."

Real smooth there. I don't know what he doesn't see in me.

I'm due back at my parents' house at one. I wish Mom didn't have to put on another big meal. John and his wife will be there. Yippee. James is still out of town. I'm the odd man—woman—out again. I sort of wish Christine would come with me. At least that way I'd have a partner.

20

I probably should have offered to cook Christmas dinner to help Mom out, but I can't fit everyone in my apartment. I don't have a dining room table anymore. Not that I even really have a dining room, but the alcove where my table should be has been converted into my work area.

And that area looks like a bomb went off. Fabric is draped and piled everywhere. On the table. Hanging off the bookshelf. Dangling from the curtain rod. Then, there are the notions. The elastic and threads and zippers. Measuring tapes and orange-handled scissors. Not to mention the containers of pins and buttons. I have a thing for buttons. I collect them like pennies. Glass jars of all sizes are filled, the cacophony of colors making me smile. I've no real organization to my buttons. Someday, when I have lots of spare time, I'll sort them by color.

That won't be today. I should try to pick up my space a little. I don't know how it's gotten this out of control. I haven't even been sewing lately. The holiday season got the best of me. I ended up working a lot more than I'd planned, which was good for my wallet. Or I should say for my creditors. My debt isn't quite as bad as it was, but it's not a good thing either. Retail is not a lucrative career.

Christine keeps telling me I should charge people for the sewing work I do for them, as well as sell my own designs. That was the plan all along. Not the alterations but the design. I've got books and books of ideas. Part of my debt, no lie, is fabric. I've got a serious addiction to fabric. I walk in a store and I lose all control. God help me if there's a sale. I've got more fabric than I will probably ever be able to use, and it's still not enough. Or it's not just right. I'll need something specific for a project, and I won't have what I need, believe it or not. That results in a trip to the store, and several hundred more dollars on my credit cards. Not a good debt-reduction system.

The last thing I sewed was a dress for Christine. She was going to some Halloween party, so I made her a gown to go as Marion, from Raiders of the Lost Ark. Of course, I didn't have the sheer white polka-dotted organza in my stock, so I made a shopping trip. Or three. The dress came out great. Christine's the perfect model, so it's easy. She's a bazillion feet tall and she teaches ballet. I don't know why she didn't pursue modeling. She never got to wear the dress, as her date—going as Indiana Jones—bailed for some lame reason or another. Too bad. They totally would have won.

Speaking of which, I wonder why she hasn't called me back. That's not like her. She's not working today, like for the first time ever. She does event planning or something like that, in addition to teaching ballet. She barely has time to sit down. She never has time for fun. I barely get to see her anymore. The last time I saw her was right after Thanksgiving. She was still working on getting through her resolution list from last January. I helped her make a cake and frosting.

I'm a freaking domestic goddess. Not that Barrett appreciates it. Obviously he doesn't. Well, I'm more like a goddess-in-training. I could be awesome, if I put my mind to it.

Now that I think of it, that's sort of the story of my life.

Like with sewing. Not just sewing—designing. I could probably make some fantastic stuff. I know what to do. I don't let myself do it.

More like I don't make myself do it. I don't really have a lot of self-discipline. That would explain the poorly paying job in a mediocre store, the boyfriend-ish fellow who is probably using me most of the time, and the mounting credit card debt due to excessive spending and aforementioned job.

Oh, I also have a little bit of ADHD. Or a large bit of it. It's a lot of work for me to stay focused. Not that I'm using that as an excuse. It's a diagnosed thing. I used to take medicine for it when I was a kid. I'm not sure why I stopped, but I'm pretty sure I'm fine without it. Nobody complains to me about my attention. At least not that I'm aware of.

Remembering that white polka-dotted organza catches my focus again. Organza is a pain to work with, but there's nothing like it. I don't have tons of that fabric left, but enough to want to make a little something. Running my fingers through the fabric, over and under the sheer slip, I start to think. I grab a piece of paper—well, a paper towel—and sketch out a blouse. The organza will make up the flutter cap sleeves and an inset panel on the front, leaving the illusion of skin between the breasts. Solid white fabric—whatever I have floating around—will comprise the front panels and the layered waist. I finish off the look with a double layer peplum.

Two hours later, I'm late for my parents', but I still have to put the zipper in the back of the blouse. I sort of wanted to finish it so I could wear it today. Sure my dad would probably comment about the sheer fabric running down the front, but it's going to look so killer with that red pencil skirt I made last summer that I don't care. Sighing, I stand up from my trusty sewing machine. My neck is cramped from being hunched over.

I'll get to wear the blouse someday.

Of course I'll need shoes to go with it. I saw a pair online a few weeks ago. If my memory serves me correctly, the hibiscus print peep-toe pumps were Louboutins, so I'll never be able to afford them. Even though being in debt doesn't seem to bother me, I can't pay more than a month's rent for one pair of shoes. No matter how perfect they might be. Even I draw the line somewhere.

My family is used to my late arrival. Have I mentioned that I am easily distracted?

Today's dinner is prime rib and roasted potatoes. My dad is the head chef for this one. Christmas Day dinner is about the only time he cooks (other than breakfast foods). The story goes that he perfected this meal to woo my mom, so she made him promise to cook it every year. Frankly, it's a pretty easy meal, and with the leftovers from last night, he doesn't have to do much.

It's weird without Lynn here, but John and James are here with their families, so it's still a full house. I thought James was out of town, but either it didn't go well or there was a change of plans. I'm not sure—someone might have said something, but I don't recall. I wasn't paying attention. A shock, I know.

"Why were you late again?" John's wife, aka Jordan, aka my arch nemesis, stares me down. My brothers are Irish twins and both about ten years older than I am. We've never been super close, and their choices in spouses sort of sealed that deal.

I've, of course, just shoved a forkful of food in my mouth. If I didn't know better, I would think she'd waited to ask the question until I would be in the most awkward position possible. Trying to chew my prime rib as quickly as possible, I hold up my index finger trying to stall. It's not the finger I want to be holding up to her, but my mom wouldn't tolerate that kind of behavior. "I was working on something."

"Oh, were you doing one of your little *craft* projects?" Her voice is dripping with sarcasm, as if my sewing were something a three-year-old would make in preschool. If for no other reason than to stick it to her, I want to be successful at design.

"Yes, of course Jordan. I was doing nothing but wasting my time and wasting my life away. What else would I be doing?"

I know I should watch my tone, but I can't. Well, I don't want to. I don't need her pointing out that my designs might as well be meaningless crafts, hobbies.

"You know, Michele, I saw something on TV the other day—I can't remember where—that they are going to have a new fashion sewing show on some channel. Kind of like that other show you like, but different sort of." Jordan looks like the cat who swallowed the canary when my mom lights up.

"Oh, Michele, that would be a fantastic opportunity for you!"

I know she's trying to be helpful, but my mom just doesn't get it. "Thanks, Mom. I'll look into it."

She knows I'm not going to look into it. I'd rather burn all my fabric than sell out for some stupid TV show.

Chapter 4

STORE CLOSED.

That's what the sign says. It's not the normal closed sign we hang at the end of business hours. It's not a special sign hung up because we didn't open yesterday on Christmas. It's a large sign, hastily scribbled on a crooked piece of cardboard, hanging in the front window, obscuring the Christmas display I'd worked so hard to perfect.

Weird.

Even weirder—my key doesn't work in the lock, which has obviously been changed since I left on Christmas Eve. I peer in through the door, and it looks like a hurricane hit the interior of U'nique Boutique. Most of the shelves have been cleared off. A vintage end table, usually used for display, lies upturned. Hangers dangle askew.

What the heck?

I start to text Mrs. Bayly but decide this is more of a phone call issue.

However, I'm not surprised that it goes to voice mail. "Um, Mrs. Bayly, it's Michele. I'm here at the store. Um, what's going on? Can you call me back? Thanks."

This is so odd. Before I can even put my phone back in my pocket, it rings. I answer without looking, assuming it's Mrs. Bayly.

"Hello."

"Oh, my God, Michele. You won't even believe this." It's not Mrs. Bayly, but my co-worker, Trinity. Trinity, the girl who was supposed to be here to open the store with me. Trinity who has more excuses for calling in or leaving early than anyone I've ever met. Trinity, the person who is a shoe-in to win a worst-decision-making contest, if there ever were one.

"What now, Trinity?" I look at my watch. The store normally opens at ten. I'm scheduled to work ten to six-thirty. Trinity was scheduled to be here for nine-thirty to open. Knowing that she's never on time, when she bothers to even show up, I arrived about twenty minutes before my scheduled start time. So, even if she were here, which she's not, Trinity would still be ten minutes late for her shift.

"Oh, my God, Michele. I can't—I don't even know where to start. I don't think, well, I think I'm going to be late today."

Considering she already is, this is not really shocking.

"What is it this time?"

Trinity's had some good excuses. I mean, there are the normal ones, like a flat tire and strep throat. But there are the creative ones, like her sister being arrested for battery, Child Protective Services being called on her, a rare viral illness that puts her out of commission one day, allows her to go get her hair done the next, and then rears its ugly head for four more consecutive days.

"Um, I've sort of been seeing this guy, and his wife found out. She went ballistic. Crazy old bat."

Right, because Trinity could never be in the wrong.

"I don't see what this has to do with work."

"Well, it's Roger."

"Roger?"

"Yeah, Roger Bayly."

"Like Mr. Bayly?" He's about seventy. Trinity is twenty-five. Eeeww. And, that might explain what's going on at the store.

"Yeah. The old bat walked in on us in the back room."

Eeeww, eeeww, double eeeww.

"She went ballistic and threw him out yesterday. She threatened to shut down the store forever."

"She didn't just threaten to. She did."

"What do you mean she did?" Trinity, need it be said, is not the sharpest tack.

"I'm here, there's a large sign that says 'store closed,' and the locks have been changed. Most of the merchandise is gone. Cleaned out."

"I can't believe the old hag did it. She said she owned it all, and she wasn't going to share it with him."

Well, I guess that explains that.

"So, did you know the store would be closed?"

"Well, not really. I mean, maybe after I left, they made up or he talked some sense into her or whatever."

Talked some sense ... what? Has Trinity lost her mind? Their lives are ruined. Their marriage, probably close to fifty years, is done. Their business, closed.

And Trinity was calling late to work, as per usual. This is shocking, even for her. Unbelievable.

Slowly, I turn away from U'nique Boutique. I don't know what else to do. It's unexpected free time. Oh, I know, I could go shopping! I bet there are a lot of after-Christmas sales. Then it sort of hits me. If the store is closed, I'm out of a job. I don't have any money coming in. I think about how my credit card bills might look like right now.

I need to sit down. I may vomit.

This is so not good.

I don't know how I'm going to pay my rent. Or electricity. Or my hairdresser.

Out comes the phone again. "Christine! Oh my God. You are not going to believe this! I can't even!"

"If it's something about Trinity, like I've said before, I don't want to hear it."

"No, this time it's not about her. Well, I guess it is." The details still have me flummoxed. Maybe that's part of what's making me want to hurl.

When I'm done, there's silence on the line. Maybe the call got cut off. "Christine? Are you still there? Hello?"

"She's outdone even herself this time."

"I know, right? But I can't decide which part of this is the most disturbing. That she was doing the nasty with him, that he was doing the nasty with her, or that now I'm up a creek without a paddle, and no money to buy one."

"Can I say D, all of the above?"

"What am I going to do?"

Christine is silent. After a few moments, I hear her sigh. "I don't have any answers. I can check and see if we have any positions open. We usually need more servers. The ones we have are not the most reliable."

Waitressing would pay the bills. At least I think it would. But it's another step away from what I want to be doing.

"I wish there were some way for me to just sew all day and have it magically pay the bills."

"You know, there are people who do that for a living." Christine's tone is dry. It's not like we've never had this conversation before. I think she's running out of patience with me.

"I've heard a rumor to that effect. My witch sister-in-law—"

"Which one?" Christine knows how much I love my sisters-in-law.

"Jordan. She, well, I think she was bating me, but at Christmas dinner, brought up this new reality show for designers and told me I should enter it. But like I said, I think it was more in a mocking way."

"Why don't you?"

"Why don't I what? Mock her? I think I do every chance I get."

"No, silly, enter the contest. At least look into it."

"Yeah, no thanks."

"Why not? You love *Project Runway*. Is it like that?"

"I don't know. And you know I'd never have the guts for something like that. I'm not good enough."

"That's bull, and you know it. You can make magic out of thin air. You should do it."

"You're right. I'm awesome."

"And humble."

"It's part of my art, darling."

"So does that mean you're going to do it?"

I think for a minute. I've made it home by now and the chaos in my dining room greets me. I've got so many bills and no way to pay them. There's a good chance I could be homeless by next month. "Sure, what else do I have to lose?"

Chapter 5

I sit, staring at the e-mail, incredulous. It can't be. Based on my application and photo portfolio, I've made it through the first two rounds already. I read through the information again. The TV show is going to be called *Made for Me*. I thought, going in, that it was much more like *Project Runway*, but it's not. Not really. Apparently, the Crown Prince of the United Republic of Montabago has found himself a bride-to-be. I'd never even heard of the United Republic of Montabago before. I'm not sure Google had even heard of it. FYI, it's a very tiny nation, almost a city-state, tucked in at the foot of the Alps. Its residents, apparently, have a long history of pomp and circumstance, and they stand on ceremony. Who knew? Anyway, Crown Prince Stephan, much to his parents' chagrin, fell in love with a commoner.

Since Maryn Medrovovich is a commoner, she dresses like one. The premise of *Made for Me* is to design a wardrobe for her first public year as the Princess of Montabago, including her wedding gown.

Shut the front door.

While I love designing and sewing all clothes in general, wedding dresses are like the Super Bowl of the fashion world. I immediately pull out my sketch pad, and pencil strokes fill the page. Page after page of ideas. I don't know if I'll be able to bring the notebook with me, if I make it all the way, but at least I'll have the ideas in my head. Hopefully.

Before I know it, it's dark in my apartment. Another day that I've lost to my process. Crap. I had a lot of stuff to get done today. Over the past few weeks, I've been selling things on Etsy to help with the bills. It isn't quite making ends meet, but at least I've had food and electricity. So far. I've got two more skirts to make to fulfill orders. My red pencil skirt has struck a chord with lots of women. I've made six in the past two weeks. The button detail down the front that creates an overlay effect with a tiny peek of thigh and lace is a selling point. At ninety-five bucks a pop, it's good money.

I force myself to crank out the last two skirts. I'll ship them out in the morning. Then, back to the email for the show. I've got to get myself organized.

They want me to come to New York City for an in-person interview. I've got to bring three to four outfits so they can see the quality. If I make it through that round, about two weeks later, I'll move into their living quarters in the city, and start the competition. Apparently, even if I'm eliminated, I have to stay on premises until the completion of the show. That way, my family won't know where I've placed. There will be ten finalists, and they expect production to take eight to ten weeks.

I don't know how I'll manage being out of my apartment for that long. Actually, I don't know how I'll continue to pay the rent. I hate to say it, but if I make it to the competition, I'm going to have to give up my place. Ugh. Twenty-nine and I'm going to have to move back in with Mom and Dad.

This is going to go over like a fart in church.

It'll probably give my mom angina that I'm not married and can't afford to live on my own. My dad will gripe and grumble about my generation but secretly will be glad I'm back under his roof. Of course, this means my social life will take a hit, and there will be no more late-night visits from Barrett.

Yes, he's visiting again. Well, he's coming over tonight.

No, we're not officially back together.

Yes, I know this is not smart.

Here's the thing. Not that we're in competition or anything, but Christine has finally found her Mr. Right. Well, she met him last January, like a year ago January, but they couldn't seem to get together all year. I don't know how you let it go that long, but that's how Christine rolls. Anyway, Christmas Eve, while I was suffering through thousands of pounds of fish and getting dropped on my keister, Christine made a late night run to Wal-Mart and ran into Patrick. That's all it took. The great romance of the century is on.

If she wasn't so blissfully happy and deserving of it, I'd be jealous.

Okay, I'm sort of jealous that she has Patrick. They really are perfect for each other and are all lovey-dovey and stuff. Seeing them together makes me lonely. Which is why I accept Barrett's visits. It's not perfect. Far from it actually. But for the little while he's here, I'm not alone.

I guess once I move back in with Mom and Dad, I won't be alone anymore. Sigh.

This is so not where I saw my life going. I think, like everyone else in my family, I expected to be married by now. I'm not sure how I saw that fitting in with my career. Truth be told, I don't know that I ever really pictured my career. Of course I always wanted to sew and design. It makes me happy. I guess I never really thought about how that works with finances and stuff. Probably because I thought my husband would work, and I could do my stuff and we'd be fine.

Except there is no husband, and I'm not fine.

The first step is to tell my parents what's going on. Like all of it. The job, the finances, the debt, the show—maybe.

Heck, even if I don't make the show, I'm probably looking at having to give up my apartment. That, or declare bankruptcy. Or both.

Since I probably won't rise to fame and fortune as the personal designer to royalty, I should come up with a life plan. Better late than never, I guess.

When I'm thinking all this in my head, it sounds a lot better and more rational than when I broach the subject to my parents over Sunday dinner.

"TV show?"

"Debt?"

"Didn't we teach you better?"

"You want to move *where*?"

"Bankruptcy?"

"The internet?"

"What happened to your savings account?"

"This wouldn't have happened if you were married."

"Where did we go wrong?"

To be honest, I stopped listening after a while. It's not like I haven't been on the receiving end of this before. I'm probably not the, um, most responsible person you've ever met. We went through this when I was in high school ... and college ... and when I dropped out of school. They'll go nuts for a while, and when the dust settles, they'll ask me what I need.

About twenty—okay thirty—minutes later, they stop. My mom looks tired. She looks that way a lot lately, which causes another wave of guilt to wash over me. I'm such a disappointment to her. I often wonder how often she wishes she stopped at three kids instead of having four. I'm fairly certain that given the age gap between Lynn and me, I wasn't planned anyway, but she won't admit it. I don't think I'm a bad person, I'm simply not a success. I'm not driven or dedicated or focused. I get it. And I don't have the drive to change any of it.

"So, do you have a plan?" My dad's tone is stern, but I know he's concerned.

"I think the best thing for me to do is to give up my apartment. That'll decrease my expenses for a while. I'm going to go down to the city to audition for the show. If I make it, I'll be there for about three months once they start production. Either way, when I'm done, I'll get another job. Christine is looking to see if she can get me in as a server where she works." Sounds totally reasonable to me.

"Well, there's one problem with that." After Mom speaks she looks at Dad for reassurance. He gives her a tight-lipped grin and nods, encouraging her to continue. "We've decided after my treatments are done and I'm totally in remission that we're selling the house. We're going to buy one of those tiny houses and spend our time traveling. We're looking to have the house sold by July or August."

After I pick my lower jaw up off the floor, I try to find words. "But you can't sell our house! What about your stuff? What about Christmas? Who's going to make all the fish? Where am I going to live?"

Dad puts his hand on Mom's, covering it gently. "The house is getting to be too much for us, especially after this year. We want to downsize. If someone else wants to take on the holiday traditions, they're more than welcome to. Otherwise, we'll rotate the big holidays between you kids, if you want us to. I've had a wake-up call, and I don't want to spend the rest of my days taking care of a house."

Looking at me sternly, Dad jumps in. "So that means you have six months to get your act together. No more. We're not keeping this house because you can't be responsible."

So not only am I about to be homeless, but I'm really about to be homeless. Oy vey.

Chapter 6

The thing about being broke is you have no money. I know that sounds obvious, but it sort of never occurred to me before. Like, I have no money coming in. Mrs. Bayly hasn't even sent me my last paycheck. Not that it was that much, since it wasn't a complete pay period, but I had been picking up extra hours. Well, that was because Trinity kept calling in. I guess now we all know why.

I managed to get out of my lease with a little smooth talking and schmoozing. That's a relief. I'd thought I could store my furniture at my parents' house, but they need the room in the garage and basement to pack and organize. With Christine and Patrick's help, I get most of the big stuff listed on garage sale sites. Makes me sick to my stomach to think of what I paid for my furniture and household items and what people are willing to pay for them. It's even worse if you consider the compounded interest I've accrued on my credit cards paying for said items.

And now, that thing with Barrett ... I still can't talk about it. Like, if Christine didn't already know, I don't think I could even tell her. It's that bad. I stuff that thought down and turn back to my prized possessions.

I can't bring myself to sell any of my sewing stuff. Not my Husqvarna sewing machine. Not my Brother serger. Not my bias tape maker. Not my fabric or notions or buttons. I want to cry as I think about not seeing my things for a while. There's only so much room in my childhood bedroom.

The cash flow from selling the contents of my life helps the finances slightly, but I still won't be able to spend tons on my trip down to New York for auditions. No riding the train in style. No taxi cabs. No fancy hotels. I have to be there about nine a.m., so I will need to go down the night before toting three to four outfits that show my design style and my sewing ability. I may need to stay for a few days, depending on how the in-person auditions go. Lucky for me, my mom's penchant for gossip—spilling the personal details of my life to her sisters—works in my favor. Aunt Maria reminds me that Tony is down in the city. Before I can even act on it, she's called him and it's all set. I can crash with him for a few days.

It takes me a while to figure out what to bring down there. The producers have been relatively tight lipped about the subject for whom we're going to be designing. My Google search only produced a black and white high school photograph of Maryn Medrovovich. There aren't a lot of answers to be found there. She's wearing the typical black cape and her hair appears medium dark. It's sort of non-descript. Which is how she looks. I can't discern her build, but I would guess medium. Maybe on the small side of medium. If she's small, that will be good for me. While most fashion designers cut clothes for supermodels, I got into sewing because I was sick of not finding clothes that fit me right. Not everyone is five-foot-eleven.

Since I can't travel down in style, I end up on the Greyhound bus. Ugh. I forgot what an unpleasant experience riding the bus is. Sitting next to strangers—why do they always want to sit next to me? And the smell. Someone always has to bring some food with a distinct odor that seeps into my nostrils, refusing to leave. I'm not sure if it's red onion or stinky feet. Either way, I wish I had a gas mask. The ride is less than four hours but feels so much longer. My eyes are dry and I have to go to the bathroom. No way in heck am I using the facilities on the bus!

Tony is supposed to meet me at Port Authority to help with my bags. I've been texting him about logistics. This is one of those times when I love being part of a large, meddling family. You need something and—poof!—someone's there, ready to help. Even when I'm complaining about my family, I can't imagine it any other way. Christine doesn't understand how or why I put up with it. She's close with her parents, but they don't live close to us. Or I should say, Christine doesn't live close to them. Either way, her parents are people she communicates with but doesn't see. Her extended family is made up of people she sees at weddings and funerals, maybe once a year.

My family is up each others' rears, but in times like this, it's certainly worth it. Tony and I agreed to meet outside the 42nd Street exit. He lives somewhere near Alphabet City. Wherever that is. To be totally honest, New York City scares me. I could never, not in a million years, drive down here. And I feel so overwhelmed in the crowds. Speaking of which, the crowd outside Port Authority is hustling and bustling. Someone bumps into me, and then I almost trip and fall over my bags. I look around for Tony but can't pick him out anywhere. It's nearly impossible for me to fish my cell out of my purse without letting go of my bags. I'm afraid if I do, someone will grab my best designs and then I'll never make the show.

"Dude, what are you doing? You look paranoid." Tony's voice in my ear startles me, making me jump.

"Jeez, don't do that to me! I thought you were trying to mug me." My fingers are cramping from their white-knuckle grip on bags.

A devilish grin spreads over his face. "Muggers don't usually announce their presence. They're much more stealth than that." He picks up my largest suitcase—the one with my designs in it and starts walking. I've got to rush to keep up with him. Good thing I wore my ballet flats. I'd never be able to walk like this in heels.

"Wait for me! Where are we going?"

"Heading to the subway. It's the fastest way."

Okay, I can do this. I cannot panic at the thought of being trapped underground. I can handle all those people, closing me in. It's one of the drawbacks of being petite. I get overwhelmed by other people very easily. I don't think most people realize it. "Tony, wait up. Don't leave me." I bustle after him and manage to survive the process. He shows me how to get a Metro card and charge it up. It's not as bad as I thought. I could possibly do this, if I had to. I wouldn't like it, but I might be able to do it.

Once back above ground, there are still about eight blocks to walk to Tony's place. Of course, it's a three-story walk up. I think if I lived down here, I'd always be in shape. The whole process of moving about the city drains me, and all I want to do is nap.

Tony has other plans. He's taking me out for pizza in Little Italy. It's another walk. Apparently everywhere you go in the city, you have to walk. My feet are killing me. I don't know how women walk around in their heels. I don't know what I'm going to do tomorrow. My outfit includes a pair of stilettos. Guess I'll toss them in my bags and wear my flats.

By the time we arrive at the tiny pizza place, my mouth is salivating from the delicious scents wafting through the air. Okay, living down here might be worth the sacrifice for the pizza. Not that we don't have good pizza Upstate, but it's not like this.

I don't understand why Tony grabs a table for four, especially when seating is so limited. My furrowed brow must tip him off because he says, "My roommates are coming."

I don't know why it didn't occur to me that Lincoln is one of Tony's roommates. Of course he is. The two are inseparable. There's another guy, Rick, as well. I don't know where they picked him up. I only wish he'd stop trying to pick me up. It's obvious that he came to dinner hoping to score tonight. I'm not being conceited. He's being very, and I mean *very* obvious. Almost bordering on Little Joey obvious.

"So," Rick drawls, "why are you down here? Tony didn't say, only that you'd be taking up residence with us."

"Well, not taking up residence. I'm staying for a night. Maybe two, if things go well."

"What things?" His accent annoys me. Normally I find a Southern accent on a guy adorable. On him not so much. It actually sounds fake. Like he uses it to pick up girls. Yuck. Rick's across from me, which isn't that great since he's trying to play footsy. I've tucked my feet up under my chair as far as I can. Double yuck. I mean, I don't want him touching me, let alone with his dirty shoes on my bare legs. Serves me right for wearing a skirt.

Tony and Lincoln seem to be taking great amusement at my expense. I'll have to remember this for the future. Maybe when Trinity is done with Mr. Bayly, I'll set her up with Tony. That would be a fun train wreck to watch.

Slick Rick, as I'm now calling him, is dominating the conversation. Despite the fact that he asked me why I'm visiting, he hasn't let me get a word in edgewise to answer. I don't know how Tony and Lincoln put up with him. It's gonna be a long night. I start wondering if Little Joey wouldn't be a better option.

Slick Rick's probably only a buck-fifty, soaking wet, so he couldn't lift me up if his life depended on it. At least tonight I won't get dropped on the floor. I mutter that under my breath. Or a little louder, since Lincoln starts laughing. "That was one of the funniest things I've seen in a while."

I elbow him, since he has the misfortune of sitting next to me. "That was not funny. That was humiliating."

Tony's laughing too. Before I can help myself, I've joined in. Slick Rick looks lost. Good. "I can't believe he dropped you."

"I can't believe my pants split!"

Despite the awkwardness provided by Slick Rick, the time passes quickly. Lincoln and Tony have me laughing the whole time. The pizza is out of this world, and I eat way more than I should. I only have one beer though. I can't afford to be hung over tomorrow.

Ugh. Just thinking about what's coming in the morning starts my nerves.

"What? What's wrong?" Lincoln seems to notice the change in my affect.

"Thinking about tomorrow and trying not to freak out."

"Where do you have to go?"

"Um, I'll have to look up the address. It's at Lifestyles Studios' home office. They're the ones putting on the show."

"Oh!" Lincoln nearly jumps out of his chair. "That's my company. They're a smaller part of Bandwidth Broadcasting."

"So do you know where I need to go?"

"Um, yeah. It's in my building. I think they're on the ninth floor. I'm on the sixteenth. What time do you have to be there?"

"I think nine. Can you show me how to get there?"

"Of course. We'll go together. I usually leave about eight, in order to account for traffic and all that stuff."

I happen to look up and Slick Rick is glaring at me. Like, glaring. Like I did something to personally offend him. What the heck? What does he want from me? Does he think that just because he's hit on me, I'll fall into his bed? I'm here for one reason and one reason only.

To get into this contest.

Chapter 7

Lincoln drops me off at the correct floor and then disappears. I'm shuttled into a hall to wait with more than twenty other wannabe stars. We've all got suitcases and garment bags. I can't help but hope that there's a steamer available once it's time to hang my stuff up. I hung it up in Tony's room last night, and it looked okay.

There are two or three garment racks that I can see. The PA, who looks about twelve, is bustling back and forth with them. We'll get to hang our things up right before it's time to go in for the final interview. I keep trying to get a glimpse of what the others have brought. The line moves slowly. No one appears to exit, so it's impossible to tell how long each person gets in there. Do they look at you, ask a question, and then they're done? Do they look over each garment carefully? Is it a personality contest?

I have to pee for about the tenth time.

I don't think I really have to go. Most likely it's just nerves. There's a little (large) part of me that's worried I'll get in there and pee my pants. That should make me nice and memorable.

"How many do you think they're going to take?"

The voice to my right startles me. I glance over at the guy next to me sprawled on the floor. He looks the epitome of relaxed. Black trousers. A fitted charcoal T-shirt. White sneakers. Huh. Bold fashion choice. Doesn't seem to matter though, because he's hot. Like superhot. Messy dark hair. Green eyes. A bold straight nose that's balanced by a Clark Kent perfect square jaw.

I'm taken aback by his perfection. "Um, as long as I'm one of them, I don't care?"

I sound like a conceited moron.

Apparently conceited morons are rewarded with a magical smile. "I like your attitude. Can we amend it to 'as long as we're one of them?'"

"Can you use 'we' with one? Somehow that doesn't seem right."

"I'm a fashion designer, not an English teacher. Sue me."

The PA comes out and hands the next rack to the green-haired person near the door. Her clothes are in black plastic trash bags. I nod toward the action at the end of the hall. "Unless she's a designer savant, I would think we have a better chance than she does. Her stuff has got to be a mess."

"She certainly doesn't spend a lot on luggage."

"Maybe it's her signature style."

"What's your signature style, One-Sixteen?"

"Sixteen?"

He nods. "Yeah, Sixteen. I'm One-Seventeen."

I look down at the number pinned to my midsection and then back at him. I shrug. "I don't have a signature style. I'm just me. I make what I feel like making."

"Did you make that?" He looks me up and down. Nervously, I smooth down my red skirt. I've changed into my black and white polka-dotted stilettos with a red bow accent. I'm wearing the white blouse I made on Christmas Day. I think I look retro but relevant all at the same time. I hope the judges agree.

"Yeah. It's hard to find stuff in the right proportions for someone my size." I'm jealous of his ability to sit comfortably on the ground. My feet are starting to hurt, but there's no way this pencil skirt will accommodate sitting on the floor.

"I'm Asher."

"Asher? Not One-Seventeen."

He grins. Holy cow. Yummy.

"Michele."

"Michele?"

"Yeah, just plain Michele. Nothing fancy or fashionable. I should probably come up with a design name."

"Or at least add an accent. Mee-chele." He overprounounces it with a French accent. He has a British accent to begin with, so his French accent makes it sound better than I ever could. I bet he could say 'donkey dung' and it would sound good. Of course he has a British accent. This kind of perfection always comes with a dashing, sexy accent.

"I don't think I can pull that off, but thanks anyway. So are we all the nine o'clock appointments? Is it this many people per hour? How many hours are we going? When do you think we'll hear?"

Asher gets to his feet. "That's an awful lot of questions, One-Sixteen, and I wish I knew. I'm risking a lot, being here."

"Oh? What's at risk?"

"I had a fight with my design partner about taking time off for this. I'm not sure he'll take me back."

"Are you successful?"

A wicked grin spreads across his face. "Tremendously."

"Then why risk it? Especially when this isn't a sure thing." I gesture to the crowd in the hall. We're moving again. The girl with the black trash bags didn't seem to be in there long.

"Because he's getting too damn possessive, and I want my own bloody voice again. Not to mention, we design menswear, and I want to break into women's wear."

I must keep a level head. Which is pretty darn hard when in the presence of such smoldering sexiness. He's not sexy. He's my competition. Nope, he's sexy too.

"Well, I've nothing to lose. Nothing at all." I know it sounds pitiful, but it's the truth. It's what happens when you're about to hit rock bottom.

The PA motions for us to move up. It's my turn to put my garments on the rack. They seemed to have fared well. I've included two dresses, a casual pants and top, and the gown I made for Christine for Halloween. I know I didn't design it per se, but the craftsmanship is exquisite, if I do say so myself. Especially the tear off part that would have allowed her to wear either the long gown, or the shortened one from after Marion is dropped in the pit of snakes.

I see Asher peeking at my stuff. It's probably nowhere near good enough to make it here. Especially not when my competition is someone like Asher, who already has his own design company. I'm sure he's not the only one. "Good luck One-Sixteen!" I hear him call.

As I head though the mysterious doorway, I'm pretty convinced that the only one I had an advantage over is the green-haired girl who had her clothes in a trash bag.

****

I'm sure I sound like a nincompoop during my audition. The highly fashionable panel of judges look bored. That's probably not a good sign. I am slightly taken aback when they ask for my design story before they ask to see the clothes. Who cares if I've got a good story—which I don't—if you have no talent? It's all about the talent. I'm not sure I have that either.

"I grew up seeing my mom and my grandmother sew. If my mom couldn't do it, she'd take it to her mother-in-law. Between the two of them, there was nothing they couldn't do. It was commonplace to have fabric on the dining room table. I watched them, in awe of how they could make a three-dimensional piece of art from a plain two-dimensional piece of fabric. By the time I was in high school, I was frustrated that clothes didn't fit me the right way. I started by altering clothes, and then finally making my own. When pressed to come up with a plan for after high school, I decided to go to design school."

"Where?" Stone-faced judge number one asks.

"Columbus School of Design, but I only lasted about a year."

"Why?" Stone-face number two this time.

"I was homesick, and then got for-real sick. Mono. I didn't handle the criticism well at that point either. Probably too immature. Too much pressure for me at that age."

They look at me. Oh crap, I bet I just shot myself in the foot.

"But that was ten years ago. I haven't stopped sewing or designing. It's really the only thing that makes me happy. It's all I want to do. I've matured quite a bit. Well, I'm working on it, certainly."

"What are you doing currently?" Back to Stone-face number one. I wonder if Stone-face number three is mute.

"I'm, uh, between opportunities. I was working at an upscale boutique but that just closed because the owner found out her husband was sleeping with one of the clerks. Not me—" I hastily add, "Another clerk. Anyway, I'm trying to figure out what to do next. I'm sort of short on cash, so I had to give up my apartment and move back in with my parents. Except they'll be downsizing this summer, and then I'll have nowhere to go. So, this is sort of my last chance to make it big before I'm out on my duff. I'm designing and selling on Etsy, but that's a long way from paying rent."

"May we see what you brought?" Number two.

Seriously? I explode with that amount of verbal diarrhea and there's not even a comment? I can't believe I've already blown it. Keeping my face neutral at this point is about as easy as making small talk during a pap smear. One by one I show them my pieces. They don't ask to hold them, or to inspect them.

There's silence in the room when I'm done. I take that as my cue to leave. I see the panel exchanging knowing glances. I bet they're going to have a good laugh about how pitiful and small town I am. That is, if they even remember who I am. All I need now is to be formally dismissed.

"One-sixteen? One last thing. Is what you're wearing one of your designs?"

I nod and do a slow spin so they can see my outfit from all angles.

They exchange looks again. Expression-less looks. I've seen zombies with more affect.

"Welcome to *Made for Me*."

Chapter 8

You know how in movies, when the heroine is excited about something, she runs and jumps into the arms of the hunky hero and it's awesome? Yeah, apparently that crap is made up. Because, when Lincoln comes to pick me up, and I run at him, he's not prepared for what I'm about to do. I elbow him in the trachea and knock him over.

Like flat on his back, in the middle of the lobby. In his place of employment. He's wheezing and gasping, and I'm struggling to get off him while still wearing my fitted skirt and heels. I accidentally step on him, almost impaling him with my stiletto. I'm so smooth.

Finally, I'm up, and I try to pull him up, you know, being the helpful sort I am. Except, even though in my head I'm helpful, in reality I'm weak as heck, and I end up falling back down on Lincoln.

I'm afraid to even look at him. I'm sure his suit is soiled to say the least. I'm going to have to pay to get it dry cleaned. I wonder how expensive that's going to be.

"Do you have a certain propensity for being on the floor or something?" Lincoln finally manages to get up, brushing himself off. He looks rumpled, but not annoyed.

"Apparently, the pull of gravity is stronger down here or something."

He smiles at me, and I can't help but laugh. Next to Lincoln's 6'2" frame, I feel like a midget.

"I take it you have good news?"

"I made it! I made the show!" I may be hopping up and down at the moment. You know, because I'm the epitome of cool.

"That's great! We've got to go out tonight and celebrate."

I look at my watch. I've been here all day. "You know, I'd love to, but there's a seven o'clock bus home. I wonder if I can catch it."

Lincoln looks at his phone for a moment, swiping through. "I'll text Tony and have him meet us at Port Authority with your stuff. That'll save time. We're not far from there now. We can grab at least a celebratory drink while we wait for him."

My watch tells me it's quarter past five. I pull up the bus schedule. The bus leaves seven-thirty. "Sure, if we make it quick."

"There's a bar right across the street. I'll have Tony meet us there."

I pop my ballet flats back on and prepare to haul my rolling bag all the way to Port Authority. Lincoln, without saying a word relieves me of the bag. "Tell me about your day."

My account takes the whole time we're walking, which seems like no time at all. Even though I've known Lincoln pretty much his whole life, it's like we're getting to know each other as people now. He asks me lots of questions, but then lets me answer. I understand why Tony likes him. He's good people.

We get to the bar and manage to squeeze into a booth. "Whatcha drinking?"

I start to pull out my wallet but Lincoln stops me. "Nope, this is on me. What'll it be?"

There's like hundreds of beers to choose from. I pick the first Belgian wheat I see, and Lincoln's off to procure our drinks. I made it. I'm going to be on *Made for Me.* TV. Me. Oh crap, I'm going to be on TV. Ten bucks says I'm going to come across like an idiot.

Tony finally arrives, about the same time the order of smothered tater tots does. Here's the thing about NYC. I could probably cook up some tots and throw some Cheeze-Whiz on them. I'd never pay fourteen bucks to do it. But, I'm hungry, and will be spending the next three hours on a bus, so who am I to refuse?

I could never live here. Too expensive. Aww, who am I kidding? I can't afford to live anywhere. What am I doing? Joining this contest is only going to delay the inevitable. Me, being bankrupt or destitute, or something equally as bad.

I let my head crash down on the table.

"Oh my God, Michele! Are you all right?" Tony's leapt up from his seat and is yanking my head back by my hair.

"Ouch!" I pull my hair out of his hand. "I was until you started mauling me. I'm just overwhelmed about life."

"But I thought you made it?"

"I made the contest. That's only the tip of the iceberg."

Lincoln leans forward. "Then what's wrong?"

"I'm in debt. Like a decent amount of debt. I have to give up my apartment, and I have no job. When this is done, unless I win, I'm going to be broke and homeless."

"Well, you need to work harder." Tony's starting to sound like his mother.

"No, duh. And you sound like your mother." Ha. I know how to hit where it hurts. None of us wants to be told we're turning into our mothers, even though they're exactly who we strive to be.

I ponder this my entire bus ride home. "You need to work harder." It echoes in my head. I work hard ... sometimes. When I have to. It's just, well, I like to do things that are easy for me. Like sewing. And maintaining a quasi-relationship with Barrett because it's easier than looking for someone new.

Look at Christine. She met Patrick last January. They played phone tag and tried time and time again to set up dates. It wasn't until Christmas Eve that they finally connected. See—that's too much work for me.

Of course, she's the happiest I've ever seen her. It's like there's a light shining from within her. And Patrick is really great. They're, like perfect for each other.

So does that mean it might take me almost a year to we get together with someone I meet today? My mind immediately flashes back to Asher. Dude, he was hawt. Like, I bet he was a model for J. Crew or something before he got into design. He seemed really nice and friendly. Flirtatious even. I'm not sure about that. Not that I'm jumping to stereotypical conclusions, but most of the best looking men in fashion won't be looking my way, if you know what I mean.

Then I think about Little Joey, and Tony's other roommate Slick Rick, and even Barrett. I'm certainly not on a winning streak here. Not in the romance department. Not really in the life department, once you consider the bigger picture.

Before I get too down in the dumps, I try to focus on the positive. Some may call me a Pollyanna. Okay, a lot of people call me Pollyanna. It doesn't bother me. My mom is doing well and her treatments are about finished. The doctors are looking to declare her cancer-free. That's certainly a positive. Lynn can now focus on getting herself knocked up. She's been trying for so long. My parents will be downsizing to a place where my dad doesn't have to spend all his free time working on things around the house. I'm not quite sure what he'll do with all his free time, but I'm guessing frequent naps will be on the docket. Not having to work at the U'nique Boutique anymore means that I don't have to deal with Trinity and all her drama. And boy, was there ever drama. That girl made some of the worst decisions ever. And repeatedly. Just talking to her used to give me angina. I don't have to deal with that anymore.

Losing my job did force me to start selling on the internet. I'd been dragging my feet about that for a while, but now that I'm doing it, it's sort of cool. I mean, there are people out there wearing Michele Nowakowski originals.

Okay, even Pollyanna can't make that name sound good. I'm going to have to come up with a name. I pull out a notebook and start writing things down. I sort of like Asher's idea of pronouncing Michele with a French accent, but I still need to do something about the last name.

I remember once my dad's aunt, whose last name was Rybaltowski telling me that they didn't even bother giving that name when they went to restaurants. Instead, she said that the last name was probably derived from the word rybak, which means fisherman, so she used the last name Fish. A quick Google search reveals that Nowakowski means "new man in town." Huh. Not a lot to work with there. New man in town. Michele Town? Michele Man? Nope—that might give people the wrong impression. Michele New? New Michele? Hmmm, I sort of like that. New Michele.

And so, on the Greyhound from New York to Albany, New Michele Designs, is officially born.

Chapter 9

The trash bag girl with the green hair's name is Kira. It fits her. Her designs must be fantastic because she made it. There are ten contestants total. We've all introduced ourselves, and I've promptly forgotten everyone's names, with the exception of Kira and, of course, Asher.

I don't think I'll ever forget him. He can be the star of my fantasies for years to come. Lord knows he has been in the two weeks since I met him at auditions.

"Good to see you, One-sixteen."

"It's Michele."

"I know. I like One-sixteen." He grins and walks away, leaving me standing there with my mouth hanging open.

About three minutes later, the perfect flirty comeback pops into my head. Dang. I should try to remember it in case I get the opportunity to use it.

Asher is across the room now, talking to a thin yet buff bald black man. They're laughing and their body language screams flirtation. Okay, maybe it's a good thing that I wasn't able to come out with my witticism. There's nothing more pitiful than a woman trying to chat up a gay guy. I should probably assume that all the males here won't be interested in me.

That's fine. I'm not here for romance. I'm here to design.

I should probably say I'm here to win, but, looking around the room, I'm fairly confident I'll be one of the first to go. I'm so ... vanilla. And while vanilla might be good in frosting, it's not going to stand out in a competition like this.

It's been an exhausting day. I came down to the city last night, crashing with Tony and Lincoln like I did for auditions last time. I barely slept at all. Tony had a friend over, and the walls in the apartment are not the thickest. Basically, I spent the entire night trying not to vomit at the sound of my cousin getting it on and wondering how they had that much stamina. From the bags under Lincoln's eyes, I think he was in a similar predicament.

This morning I took a cab to the apartments provided by the show, and then was shuttled to the studios. The production team is now filling us in on the schedule. We haven't seen the design room yet. In my head I'm picturing something like *Project Runway*. That would make sense. The assistant to the producer is droning on and on. I know I should be paying attention, but I'm too busy sizing up the competition. Asher notices me looking around the room and he winks.

Huh.

I snap my focus back to the production people. Again, I can't remember their names. Would it be too much to ask for everyone to wear name tags? Then I realize she's talking about the timeline. I guess I really thought that each "challenge" was spread out over a week.

"You need to clear your mind from any preconceived notions. This is not *Project Runway*. We do not have challenges. We have assignments. Each assignment will serve a specific purpose for Duchess Maryn."

The eclectic woman sitting next to me leans over. "I thought she was a princess?"

I shrug. I would think she won't officially be a princess until she gets married, but what do I know about the royal family of Montabago? Until this show came up, I'd never even heard of Montabago. "Maybe she's a duchess until the wedding?"

"Oh right, makes sense. Who are you again?"

"Michele."

"Oh right. The plain one. I'm Fink."

It's on the tip of my tongue to reply that she has an unfortunate name, but I somehow manage to bite it back.

The producer continues. "Your first assignment will be given tomorrow. Until then, we ask that you don't leave the apartments. After you each left your things there earlier today, we divided you up as we chose. Good luck and happy designing!"

We're shuttled back to the apartments. There are two with five occupants in each. I guess I am the plain vanilla one, as I'm slightly taken aback that the division is not based on gender. My apartment-mates include Kira, Butch, Fink, and Asher. Lexington, Sancere, Gordon, Weyler, and Breckyn make up the other suite. A large common space connects the two apartments, so there's no real division. Lexington is the fellow with whom Asher was cozying up earlier. If I had to guess, I would think that Sancere is trans female. She's certainly got better legs than I do.

Kira and I end up in a room together. My choice was her or Fink, but I don't think I'm a fan of hers. I'm liberal, but I don't know that I'm quite liberal enough to share a room with a man, which narrows my choices. I mean, I guess it would be okay. Unless it was Asher, and then it would be hell. I need to watch myself, especially when the cameras are rolling. I'm sure they'll be looking for drama. Like I said, I'm pretty plain and low key, so I bet they'd love to catch me mooning after the unavailable man in my apartment.

After we're settled, some staff from the show bring in trays of food. I guess we're not allowed to leave the premises for a while. We're sprawling out in the common area between the two apartments, all ten of us. There's a lot of trying to out-flamboyant each other. I've got nothing to flamboy, so I just take it all in.

The crowd is eclectic and eccentric, and for all its oddities, stereotypical. You've got Kira with the green hair. Fink with her leather corset and coal black eyeliner. Lexington is the drama queen. Butch is the ironic hipster and is ironically not butch. But in an ironic way. Breckyn and Weyler are the fashionistas. Gordon is also gay, but middle aged. He sort of reminds me of Isaac Mizrahi. Sancere is definitely trans, as she's mentioned it no less than ten times in as many minutes. That leaves Asher and me.

Questions are being bandied about. I'm tired and on my fourth glass of wine, and it's hard for me to pay attention. Not like it's ever easy.

"Has anyone seen a recent picture of Maryn?"

"What size is she?"

"What events are we going to have?"

"I already have her wedding gown planned out."

That last comment is from Gordon.

I want to chime in that my understanding of the contest is that we're supposed to match *her* personal style, not the other way around. That's fine with me. If he's coming in with everything set in his head, there's a good chance he'll be eliminated in an early round.

Fine by me.

I've got some sketches with me, certainly. Some things from my archives, as well as new material, no pun intended. I do keep having visions of wedding gowns, but they're for Christine. Not that she and Patrick are engaged yet, but anyone with eyes can see it's coming. I'll have to convince her to let me make her gown. But that's another issue for another day. The wine and the stress of the day are sapping my ability to keep my eyes open, so I inform the crowd that I'm heading to bed.

As I leave the room, I hear, "What a dud. Can't wait until she leaves so the fun can really start." If I had to guess, I'd say it was Fink. Rat-Fink, if you ask me.

I try not to let it bother me. I'm here to do a job.

****

Laugh all you want, but with the five a.m. wake-up call, I'm the first out of bed and ready to go. I've got plenty of time to primp and preen and make sure I look good for the cameras. There're a lot of puffy eyes, shuffling walks and, I would guess, headaches, if the

64

number of spent wine bottles is any indication. The production crew of about six is here to film us as we embark on our first day—the first assignment. I know it's going to be a long day. They've explained that to us. They've also explained that stopping to eat will be mandatory, along with sleeping at night.

You don't have to tell me twice. It's easy for me to lose track of time when I'm working, for sure, but I need my sleep. Sleep is very important in my life. Always has been. Always will be.

Not surprisingly, it takes the crew of divas quite a long time to put themselves together. I always thought I was high maintenance. I'm nothing compared to this crew. Sitting around and waiting gets boring. There's no TV, no computers, no phones. We're cut off from the internet and anything fun. I grab a bagel and bowl of fruit and wait. And wait. And wait. What I wouldn't do for a crossword puzzle book. And I don't even like crosswords.

Asher joins me eventually. "How long do you think this is going to take?"

I shrug. "Sancere still has a way to go to get her face on, but I think Butch may take longer getting ready. Coffee?" I hand him a mug.

"Thanks. I have the feeling this will be the first of many today. What do you think our assignment is going to be?"

"Well, I would hope that we'd get to meet Maryn first. You know, talk to her. Get a feel for what she wants and needs."

"Wouldn't it be bloody brilliant if they had us do this first challenge—I mean *assignment*—without meeting her first?"

Apparently we're bloody clairvoyant, because that's exactly what happens.

When the crew is finally all pulled together, we're shuttled to the studio where we're herded into a dark room. I stumble along, tripping on cords before finally finding my seat. Great. I thought I was going to be the stereotypical good girl on the show, but I guess my role will be the buffoon instead.

Callie Smalls steps out across the room, illuminated by soft lights. She is breathtaking. The supermodel is thinner than I ever imagined. I'm in awe of being in the presence of a celebrity. Glancing out the corners of my eyes, I try to see if any of my fellow contestants are star struck. Nope, just me. Fink is staring at her fingernails, oblivious to our host. Weyler and Breckyn are looking her up and down, probably critiquing something. Gordon is giving her a little wave with his fingers in a familiar way.

I so do not belong here.

I need to focus on the goal. Heck, my goal isn't even to win. It's simply to gain exposure for my Etsy store so that I can pay rent. That's not too much to ask. I figure I need to sell about twenty pieces a month to survive. Not to live extravagantly, but to survive. Surely being on a TV show will give me that. I'll probably need to have more of a social media presence. I wonder if Christine will help me with that. If only I could call her and ask. Damn media blackout!

My runaway train of thoughts is interrupted by the sudden clapping of my fellow contestants. I missed everything Callie Smalls just said. Ooops. I really should focus.

Callie waits for the soundman to adjust something and then continues. "The first assignment will be a blind assignment. You'll be given measurements but won't meet Duchess Maryn until the presentation."

You could hear a pin drop. We're supposed to design specifically for a person we've never met, never even seen? It's all luck. Crapola.

"You'll be creating a day outfit for Duchess Maryn to wear while she conducts a press interview. It will be her first appearance after the official engagement. Up to this point, the duchess has been out of the public spotlight. The engagement will be announced, and then she will do this one media event. Most Montabagans are aware of her, but not of the seriousness of her relationship with Prince Stephan. You will have two-hundred dollars to spend, and this outfit must be ready for show tomorrow afternoon."

I glance at my watch. It's ten a.m. already. That doesn't leave tons of time. My mind is already whirring. I wonder what the measurements are going to be. That will change how the design looks and feels. It will need to be something über flattering from all angles.

The cameras shut off, and the production crews start splitting us up.

"What's this?" Lexington leans over to me and whispers. Well, as quietly as he can. He's definitely the loud sort. He'd fit in well at my house. His skin reminds me of smooth milk chocolate, and suddenly I'm craving a Hershey bar. I wonder if craft services would take requests.

I need to answer Lexington. "I dunno. Why are they leading us off two by two? Are we heading to an ark?"

My name is called in the next group, so I'm about to find out. It's an interview, getting our feelings and impressions before we start our first assignment. My stomach clenches and I'm sweating like I've just finished Zumba. I'm sure that will look good on camera. Luckily, someone swoops in and powders my face. The PA instructs me to talk to the camera, like it's a person, as she hooks up my microphone.

"Ready?" she asks. I try to swallow the cotton balls that suddenly fill my throat. I can only nod in response. I don't have a good feeling about this.

"Tell me how you feel about the first assignment."

It's like being on a shrink's couch.

"I, um, well, um, aaaah ..."

"Stop." The suddenness to her tone makes me jump. Great. I've already colossally screwed this one up. "Michele, you've got to relax. Who's your best friend?"

"Christine."

"Okay, then pretend the camera is Christine. What would you say to her about this assignment? What are you feeling? What are your thoughts about the competition?"

"I'm about to freak out about being on camera and making a jerk out of myself. Which, I think I've just accomplished."

The PA smiles and nods, encouraging me to continue.

"Obviously I'm nervous. What if I freeze? What if I have no ideas? What if I have too many ideas? Sometimes I have issues with focus. Like right about now. And then I worry that I won't get the style right. I mean, I have my style. I have what I like to make. What if it's not her style?"

"How would you describe your style?"

"Um, inspired by my grandmother. Fifties and sixties, but with a current angle."

"Relevant retro?"

I have to laugh. "See? That's another thing. I'm not good with things like that. I flunked out of design school, mostly because I wasn't cool enough. I'm much more like your grandmother's designer than a hip designer."

They smile and nod, and shoo me on my way. And now I know what my sound bite for the intro episode will be. Ugh. Suddenly, I feel the need to eat my weight in pastries.

Chapter 10

You've got to be kidding me. Save for the difference of about five pounds (in my favor, thank you very much), the duchess' measurements are virtually the same as mine. She's a short girl too.

Huzzah for the littles.

I'll bet my weight in cannolis that the wedding dress good-ole Gordo already designed is based upon her height being about five-foot-eleven and a size two. You know, perfect for a supermodel. Disastrous for the petite set like myself.

We still don't know her age, which should ultimately influence our designs. We're in the thirty-minute design period. After this, we'll get our fabric and notions. I'm mentally going through some of the ideas I've had. This has to be assignment specific too. You would think the design room would be silent, but apparently singing softly—or not so softly—is what helps Kira, and Lexington talks to himself. Breckyn keeps looking around frantically, and scratching out items on her page even more frantically.

My page is blank. That's because I'm thinking. My usual process is that I find the fabric first and then come up with a design. I don't know if that strategy is going to work this time. Okay, she's doing a media event. Will she be sitting? Will she be standing? Will she be doing both? It's got to be a fabric that won't wrinkle as she sits. Just like that, I've eliminated a whole bunch of fabrics.

I decide to go with a jersey knit. I know, bold choice, since it can show every bump and roll. But when used right, it can be forgiving and won't wrinkle. And it will have to be a solid color. Prints can look funky on TV. Now to design it. It'll need to be well-constructed and novel without having any weirdness that will leave the TV audience squinting at their set trying to figure out what they're looking at.

An idea comes to me, and I begin sketching. Use of darting and piping will give the jersey some structure. I go with a modest design. I'd rather err on the side of caution, at least in round one. The ideas are solidifying in my head faster than I can get them on paper. It's a good thing. Off to the fabric store.

I feel like a kid in a candy store. Those contestants who live here in New York City, especially those who went to FIT have undoubtedly been here before. Despite the fact that I only live one-hundred and fifty miles away, I might as well still have straw in my hair. JoAnn's House of Fabrics has nothing on this place. Three floors of fabric, stacked floor to ceiling. When the show is over, I'm booking a week's vacation and spending it here.

I need to focus.

"Wipe the drool from your mouth." Asher's voice breaks up my reverie.

"Do you think they'd let me stay here once the show is done?"

"I think you'd get lost and never come out."

"But I'd die happy, surrounded by all this fabric." I think from now on, I may have fantasies about this store. Asher may have a roll in them as well. Kira darts in front of us, causing me to remember why I'm here.

"I should get to work," I tell him, starting to walk away.

"Do you know what you're looking for?" Is he fishing for help?

"I think so. I've a general idea. Catch you on the flip side!" With that, I'm off, running up and down the aisles. I find a dark magenta, almost plum, jersey knit that will work. Black for the piping and trim. Lining material, interfacing in case I need to stiffen it up. A zipper and thread. And then I see the button section. I swear, if it was possible, I'd have an orgasm right here and now. So. Many. Buttons.

This is it. I've found heaven. I root through and find interesting black buttons to trim my dress. I hear Weyler call out that we have ten minutes left. Mentally adding my totals, I've got plenty to spare. I dash back and grab some black suiting material to make a little jacket to go over the dress. The duchess may be self-conscious about her arms, so this will give her options.

While waiting to have my fabric cut, I start to panic. What if this isn't a good color on her? What if it's too blah? I jump out of line and dash back to where I pulled the fabric originally. This time, I pull navy for the dress, aqua for the piping, and find a very subtle print that ads a pop of color for the jacket. Even better because there are buttons in the exact shade of aqua that I need that almost look like jewels. They'll give even more pop, without being gaudy or over the top.

I check out, still middle of the pack. I've a few dollars left. I'm tempted to buy more buttons, but I doubt I'll be able to keep the excess when I'm done. Man, how awesome would that be?

On the shuttle back to the design studio, my cast mates are abuzz with excitement. I am too. My fingers are itching to get sewing. Not only that, but I'm interested to see what everyone else comes up with. You know, size up the competition.

As I think that, my gaze involuntarily slides over to Asher. He's sitting next to Lexington. Weird. Every time I think he's sort of flirting with me, the next thing I know he's flirting with Lexington. The last thing I need is to waste energy on someone who's unavailable. I did enough of that with Barrett Snyder the rat. That's his full name now, Barrett Snyder the rat. I say it like it's all one word, "BarretSyndertherat." He was given that title when, the night after the last time he visited me, he booked his wedding. At Christine's place of business. That's right, Christine will be planning and catering his wedding. I guess his fiancée doesn't know about our on-again, off-again relationship. You know, I'd been having a bad enough time that week. It was the last thing I needed to hear. Apparently, as I was calling Barrett, leaving that stupid message, he was with *her*, at *her family's* house, proposing. I guess only some families scare him away. Or maybe it was just me. Of course, that didn't stop him from coming over. Either way, he's a rat, and I've got to focus on the task at hand.

Designing and creating the most perfect interview dress for someone I've never met.

Draping knit is not the easiest task in the world. Before I start, I double check the measurements on my dress form. Seems amateur, I know, but I'm making clothes for a real person. I'm worried that the bust won't be right. According to the measurements we got, she's a 34-C. That doesn't sound big, but she's 5'1". Her girls are going to play a prominent role. I look around my table. A-ha! Grabbing some of the batting I picked up to make the piping, I fashion, well, breasts. I use the muslin provided to us to make a bra-type apparatus, and then slide the batting in. It takes time because no one wants lumpy boobs.

I step back and admire my handy work. But then I glance around the workroom. It's silent—you could hear a pin drop. Literally. There's fabric being draped and cut. And all I have are boobs.

I start draping and pinning and marking my fabric. There is a top piece, which is a front and back that will be connected under the arms, and a skirt piece, attached at the waist. The dress is going to look like one side wraps over the other with the contrasting piping trim.

Did I mention piping is a pain in the tuchas to make? Mental note—no more custom piping. I plan to line the piping with a row of buttons. I've got to include the buttons. They're my signature. Well, if I had a signature that is. They are on the logo for New Michele Designs, so I guess they are officially my signature.

My concentration (woo hoo for finally being able to concentrate on something!) is broken by one of the PA's announcing that we'll be taking breaks for dinner.

I squint up at the clock, my eyes tired after doing such close work for so long. It's almost six! Where did the day go? Then I look about the room. There are crews walking about, I guess filming. There's a lot of action going on, but not much *action* from a TV standpoint.

Almost everyone has something draped on his or her dress form. There are a lot of suits going on. Pant suits and skirt suits. I count ... one ... two ... three ... four suits. That means forty-percent of contestants are presenting this look. Huh. Either I'm wrong or they are. There's a lot of bright fabric and flower prints. Bold flower prints. Heavy fabrics. Lots of tailoring going on. Well, except for Sancere, who has a long, flowy dress. Gordon's dress is low cut. Like J-Lo low. Did he not read her measurements? Her girls are going to be on display for the world to see. Probably not what the future princess is going for.

Or maybe I'm wrong.

It's happened before.

Looking around the room again, the pit in my stomach grows. I'm so out of my league here. Why did I ever think this was a good idea? Couldn't the casting people see what a disaster this is going to be? I'm going to be humiliated on national TV.

Breckyn and I head out to lunch. She's one of the suit-ers. It's a smart-looking piece, I'll give her that. Craft services has outdone themselves this time. If I last on this show (a big if at the moment), I'm probably going to gain ten pounds. There are salads and sandwiches and, oh, just so much food.

I'm tempted to take a tuna salad roll-up, but I'm hesitant about two things: the possibility of food poisoning and having bad breath for the rest of the day. I settle on a roast beef sandwich, pasta salad, and a nice tossed salad. There's the Italian in me, coming out again. Referring to my food as nice. Aunt Maria is famous for it ("I make you some nice chicken and some nice ziti." Like she would serve crappy food).

Suddenly, I miss my family. I've only been away two days, but it's the forced radio silence that gets to me—knowing I can't talk to them, even if I want. Wondering how Mom is feeling. How Lynn is doing with her fertility issues. The doctors decided that maybe they'll need a little help getting pregnant, and she's taking it hard. What Christine and Patrick are up to. Even what Tony and Lincoln are doing. Well, Lincoln's probably in the same building as I am. I wonder if I'll run into him in some of our comings and goings. It's all I can do to blink back the tears.

For the love of Pete, it's day one of competition. If I don't steel my nerves now, I'll crack like an egg before this assignment is over.

Chapter 11

I'm amazed at what can happen in a few hours. My dress is nearly complete. Instead of a traditional blazer, I decided to make a cape blazer. It's got the shoulder structure and lapels of a suit coat, but there are panels down the front, split for the arms and hands to go through. The back has more material to it, like a cape. Hence the name. I've made it out of the navy suiting material, as the jersey knit would be too loose and wouldn't hold proper shape. Along the lapels, I added a contrast print to give a pop of color, along with more of the aqua piping. I made all the blasted stuff. I might as well use it.

It's eleven o'clock and my eyes feel like I've rubbed them with sandpaper. The adrenaline ran out about forty-five minutes ago. I can't wait to go home, well, back to the apartments, and go to bed. Tomorrow we'll get about two hours after the fitting to perfect the look, and then the unveiling will occur. Not unlike that other show, we get to have input into how our models will be styled. It'll be interesting to have that many short busty girls in one room. After seeing some of the other outfits, I think people are going to be in for a big surprise when it comes to proportions.

Tee hee.

When we get back to the apartments, it turns out some of the others are as keyed up as I am tired. More wine appears. You'd think the show's producers would know better. Maybe they do, and this is what makes for good TV.

I should try to be social. Lexington is quite funny, as is Kira in a dry way. Gordon and Butch go for shock value, but Sancere wins, hands down. She's got stories upon her stories. She should write a book. I know that because she keeps saying, "Sugar, I should write a book."

One more glass of wine and then I'll go to bed. As I'm pouring it, Asher slides up next to me. "How you feeling?"

Holding up the glass I shrug. "I dunno. I'm still not sure of what to expect. I think, after tomorrow, it'll be easier, because we'll know what's coming. Right?"

It's his turn to shrug. "I wonder how many surprises and twists they'll throw at us. Like, will we have to make an outfit out of newspapers or CD's or something?"

Taking a sip, I get the courage to look directly at him. Damn, he is fine looking. Do you think he'd mind if I licked him? Focus. "You seem nervous. Surely you can't be nervous. You're already an established designer!"

He takes a sip. We're standing in a corner of the kitchen and because people keep walking by, we've inched closer and closer together. "Of course I'm nervous. Aren't you?"

"Well, yeah. Duh. But I'm such a newbie. I sew. I make clothes for fun. I couldn't even hack design school. You have your own company. You, like, make money with your clothes already. You're going to be a star."

He smiles. "Oh, you shameless flirt, padding my ego. Trying to distract me from being in this competition." Asher reaches out and rubs my arm. It's all I can do not to drop my glass of wine.

"No, I'm not flirting. I'm being serious. I think you have a distinct advantage over a lot of people here, namely me."

"No, darling, that's where you've got it wrong. You design women's clothes. Right there, you have one up on me. Secondly, what if my partner is truly the talent and the inspiration of the company? We've been together so long, it's hard to tell where he stops and I begin."

Now, I know I should be focused on what he's talking about in terms of design and whatnot, but all I can do is wonder about his partner. Maybe this glass of wine wasn't a good idea, because before I know it, I hear those words coming out of my mouth. "How much of a partner is he to you?"

Asher smiles, one of those wicked smiles. "Trying to feel me out, love?"

Blush, ruby, scarlet, crimson, blood. These are the shades of red I imagine my face is turning about now. "I, um, you know, just wondering. Most of the people here ..." I gesture out toward the common area, "... it's easy to tell. With you, not so much."

That wicked grin again. "That's the way I like it. Keep 'em guessing."

"Well, that tells me nothing."

He leans in and whispers in my ear, his breath hot against my skin. "I go where the mood takes me, love. Whatever—whoever—strikes my fancy at any given moment." And with that, he turns and walks away.

Huh.

That's probably a complication I don't need at the moment.

Rather than rejoin the crowd, I finish my wine and head to my room. Kira's already in there, in bed.

"Sorry. I'll be quick," I say as I grab my things to go change. Once I'm in my jammies and my face is scrubbed clean, I dart back into our room and slide into bed. Aaaahhhhh. It feels so good to lay down. I may let out an involuntary groan.

"Do you think they'll bring massage therapists to the set? It's day one and everything is tight and tired. I can't imagine what it will get like."

"That would be heaven. I'm so tense. I've got so much to finish." Kira's voice is soft. I can hear the worry in it. I feel her pain.

"I know, me too. What do you have left to do?"

She tells me the finishing details that need to be completed on her jumpsuit. It's a fashion forward piece, and from what I saw, the construction is impeccable.

"I've got to hem both the dress and the cape blazer and put the buttons on the dress."

"That doesn't seem too bad. You'll be fine."

"I hope. Then, it'll all come down to a matter of taste." I think back to the outfits I saw today. Mine is definitely more on the conservative side, which is funny because I never thought of myself that way.

"In this moment, it's like everyone's totally equal, because we don't know what she's like, or what she's going to like."

Kira's words hang in the air as I drift off into a fitful sleep.

Somehow, the five a.m. wakeup call is a lot more harsh the second day. I think hateful thoughts at the producers as I stumble out of bed and try to get ready. I make sure to eat a good breakfast, since who knows when our lunch will be. I grab an extra apple and throw it in my bag, just in case. Yesterday, we were too busy to think about being hungry. I'm sure we're in for more of the same.

The first two hours in the design room are spent finishing up and fitting our models. I'm very happy with the way my dress and cape came out. Stylish, sophisticated, with a hint of vintage glamour. Plus buttons.

I have the hairstylists put my model's hair in low chignon, á la Grace Kelly. If it worked for one princess, it should work for another, right? I add bright magenta peep toe slingbacks, picking up the color of the print in the lapel. I find some chunky but elegant earrings.

There's a mad panic about the design room as we all finish up. It's like mice scurrying about. There are the ten designers, ten models, and double the normal film crew. There are more people in black T-shirts than anyone else, and they seem to be trying to stay out of the way. Not necessarily successfully, but not totally imposing.

Before I know it, we're being whisked up in the elevators to the room where we'll have our presentations. Not dissimilar to a runway show, but we certainly can't call it that. We need something more fitting and more regal.

The studio where we were yesterday morning has been absolutely transformed. The production staff is now referring to it as the "presentation room." Whatever floats their boats. Plush carpets line the floors. The walls are covered in a subtle, yet expensive-looking brocade wallpaper. The tones of the room are soft creams and blues and gold. It's almost like a super-posh bridal studio, with mirrors positioned in a tri-fold way, of course framed in gold guilding. We're ushered into blue upholstered King Louis side chairs. Much nicer than the folding chairs we were in yesterday. I half expect them to serve us flutes of champagne. The only issue is that the room is freezing. I'm wishing I'd worn a sweater. Or a winter parka.

Callie Smalls steps out in a stunning royal blue gown. I wonder who her designer is. The production crew descends and hooks up her mike. Her hair is primped and makeup blotted, not that it needed to be. Then, we're all wired for sound. There are three empty chairs on the other side of the studio. I wonder who will be sitting in those.

My nerves are consuming me. If they don't get this underway, I may barf. I glance at Breckyn, who's sitting to my left. She's wringing her hands in her lap. Lexington, to my right, is tapping his foot incessantly. Glad to know it's not just me. Callie's face is still and expressionless. Makes me wonder if she's had a whole lot of Botox or something. The crew adjusts the lights for the millionth time. The room has gotten exponentially warmer since the lights blazed on. Guess

I'm glad I left the parka at home. But I could use some water. Or maybe not, since I've got to pee again. It's the nervous pee. Again. If they don't get this show on the road pretty soon, I think I'm going to combust.

Chapter 12

"Welcome to the inaugural episode of *Made for Me*. I'm your host, Callie Smalls. Starting tonight, we'll be watching ten of the best up-and-coming fashion designers compete to become the personal designer for Duchess Maryn Medrovovich. Duchess Maryn has been living a life out of the public spotlight. At this time, she's ready to make her debut. Well, almost ready. Our designers have been tasked with making the duchess' media presentation outfit. They've yet to meet the duchess. Rather, they've designed blind. We provided them with Duchess Maryn's measurements, and that is all."

Callie Smalls pauses and smiles at the camera. I think I've forgotten even to breathe while she's been speaking. She's so tall and eloquent. You know, the antithesis of me.

"Tonight, creations from all ten designers will be presented. Following deliberation, Duchess Maryn will make her media debut wearing the chosen look."

There's a collective gasp from the contestants. Well, maybe it was just me, but I felt like the others were gasping with me. Suddenly, it's not about trying to get some extra business that I want. I want to see the duchess in one, or more, of my dresses. I want to go all the way to the end and design her wedding dress.

Callie Smalls stops talking and the sound guy filming her indicates that they're stopping the cameras. Callie delicately picks her way from the center of the stage, in front of the mirrors to the three chairs across from us. Taliance Ho, the acclaimed wedding gown designer, makes his way in and sits next to Callie. The last chair remains empty.

"Do you think that's Maryn's seat?"

I'm surprised at Lexington's casual tone in referencing the duchess. I wonder if we'll be told how we should address her. I've never personally spoken to a member of any royal family before. Heck, the closest I've ever come to royalty is getting a whopper from Burger King. I'm pretty sure I'll manage to mess it up when the time comes. Assuming I make it through tonight.

There's more shuffling of the cameras and lights, and then the show begins. They put on some music, I assume to give the models a beat to walk to. If that's how it works. I'm 5'1". My knowledge of runway comes entirely from binge watching *America's Next Top Model*. And how bitter was I when they had the short girl season, and most of them were still like 5'6". That's totally not short. Anyway, the first look comes out. It's Asher's.

I am so out of my league. It's a soft dove gray dress. I think it's actually a very subtle plaid, but it looks like a solid from a distance. It has cap sleeves, a boat neck, and a dropped waist. There's a waistband, which makes the model's waist look infinitely small. The skirt is pleated, and the overall look is super flattering. Most of the time, short girls can't wear pleats because the skirts are too long. Asher has hemmed his to the perfect length. There's a matching suit coat. He and I were thinking along the same lines. He's styled it with classic black pumps and pearls. As much as I love the dress (and I seriously do), I don't love his styling. I should give him pointers. Well, I would if we weren't in competition.

Gordon's look is next. To me it's a total miss, but we won't know until we meet the duchess. Like I predicted, the girls are on full display. We don't even know how old the duchess is. If she's over thirty, I'd bet they're going to be hanging low, and this won't be flattering.

We don't know the order, so every time a model steps out, it's like playing Russian roulette. My dress finally comes out, eighth. Freakin' eighth. It's torture to wait all that time.

And from the moment my model steps out, breath escapes me. I absolutely love my look. She's classy and collected, but cool. Relevant retro indeed. And while I want to go all the way, I don't know that I'll ever feel more proud than I do right here in this moment. I hope my grandmother is looking down on me.

Asher leans forward. "Stunning, love. You nailed it. Love the buttons."

As soon as the show is over, we're ushered into another room where we wait. And wait. And wait. At some point they bring food in. I mindlessly graze, too anxious to fill a plate, but too nervous to stop eating. We're still all mic'd up, and there's a crew in here filming us. Someone asks how long this is going to take, to which the answer is a shrug.

We're allowed to take bathroom breaks, but that's about it. And when we do, we're escorted by a production member. Like they're afraid we're going to sneak into the deliberation or something. Which isn't a bad idea. The suspense is killing me.

I try to talk myself down. It's not like this is a big deal. Just my entire future, that's all.

The conversation in the side room gets raucous, as it's bound to do with this cast of characters. I don't feel like I have much to add, but I enjoy the show. Other than Fink. She's still more on the nasty side than anything else. Lexington is hysterical. I can see why Asher is drawn to him. But he also seems drawn to me as well. I'm so confused.

After what seems like years, but is, in fact, only four hours, we're quietly ushered back into the presentation room. A large object covered in a sheet has been moved into the room, over by the mirrors. If I had to guess, I'd think it was a garment rack. We all shuffle back into our seats. Callie Smalls is back out and is getting touched up. Taliance Ho is back in his seat. The third blue King Louis chair remains vacant.

After a nod from the head cameraman, Callie begins. "After careful deliberation, which included Duchess Maryn trying on all the garments, the first round picks have been made. Tonight, one designer will be asked to leave, while another designer will make his or her debut as Duchess Maryn and Prince Stephan give their first media interview. Tonight."

I glance down the row and see the absolute panic on Sancere's face. I mouth "what" to her. She leans over Butch and Lexington to whisper, "I sewed my model in her dress. I was having zipper issues. There's no way the duchess could have gotten the dress on or off. I'm doomed!"

Oh crap. She's probably right. We had no idea the duchess would actually be trying the garments on, let alone wearing them for her debut *right now*. This is certainly an unexpected twist.

Callie continues. "On this rack are the three looks for which the duchess did not care. From these three looks, one designer will make his or her royal exit. Judging criteria included fit, construction, and overall taste. And now, the three lacking looks."

Ouch. That's a harsh way to put it. My face winces involuntarily. My hands are gripping the front edge of my chair as I'm leaning forward. I cross my fingers and scrunch my eyes shut. I can't bear to look as Callie steps over to the rack. With a flourish that makes me wonder how many times she practiced disrobing the garment rack, Callie removes the covering. Hanging forlornly on the rack are the designs by Gordon, Breckyn, and Sancere.

I'm not on the rack.

The air whooshes out of my chest in relief. I sink back into my chair. I feel badly for Sancere. She's about to lose it. I don't understand why Breckyn's suit is on the rack. It's a fine suit. Black. Respectable. Seems to be aptly constructed. I'm not at all surprised about Gordon's look. I like Sancere, so I'm rooting for Gordon to go home. He's arrogant, and I don't like that. Sancere's dress is beautiful. Other than the zipper issue, I'm not sure it's appropriate for the occasion. More like a gown for an evening event. I wonder what went wrong with the zipper, because the rest seems well put together. If she makes it through, I'll ask her.

After enough time has passed to make sure the three at-risk designers are nice and uncomfortable, Callie continues. "Breckyn, your design was found to be boring and predictable. However, you will remain on the rack."

The cameras tighten in on her to get her reaction. I don't know how her look could be predictable, when we don't even know the person for whom we're designing. But anyway, she's safe, so that's good.

Callie's again center stage. "That leaves Gordon and Sancere. Please come forward."

Oh, dang. This is harsh. They make you get up and stand front and center to humiliate you. I want to throw up on behalf of both of them. They make their way up and stand side by side. Callie smiles. It only reaches the corners of her mouth. I don't think the rest of her face moves.

"Gordon, your look is on the rack because it showed a lack of taste and modesty. Duchess Maryn felt that she was too exposed, especially for someone in her position."

Callie focuses on Sancere. She's sweating through her copious layers of make-up. I want to throw up for her. "Sancere, there were significant issues with construction of your dress." She pauses, waiting for Sancere to answer.

"Um, yes. I had zipper issues. It was buckling the fabric, so rather than putting the zipper in, I sewed my model into the dress."

"Which then rendered the garment unwearable by Duchess Maryn. There was also the question of appropriateness for this event. On a positive note, the duchess did appreciate the design and flow of this dress, if for another event."

Sancere drops her head. She's struggling not to cry. I hope to God I'm never up there, although odds are pretty good that I will be up there someday soon.

Callie looks sternly at the two. "Tonight, the contestant who's not fit to stay on the rack is ..."

Have I ever mentioned how much I hate dramatic pauses?

"Gordon."

He hangs his head as Sancere bursts out in tears. Well, at least I'm not the first on the show to cry.

Gordon is ushered out and Sancere tearfully returns to her chair. Her makeup is a mess. I hope the cameras don't zoom in too closely on her right now.

Callie's center stage again. "Duchess Maryn has chosen her top three looks. She will retain them for her personal use, although she has the right not to use them. She is wearing her favorite look, as designed and styled by the contestant. Now, without further ado, the third favorite look is ...

Chapter 13

Again with the dramatic pauses. I think by the time I'm done on this season I'll have a serious issue with dramatic pauses. And it's only the first show. Ugh.

Callie crosses to the left side of the stage. There's what I would guess to be a dress form, covered in a sheet. There's a matching one on the right side of the stage as well. With a perfect flourish, Callie unveils the third place look. It's Lexington's.

My throat clenches. I don't know why. I'm safe for tonight. Nothing else should matter. Except now, for the first time, I really want this. Like, I *really* want it. More than I ever wanted anything. I'm prepared to fight for it.

I should congratulate Lexington, but I can't. I can't move. I wish I could push fast forward and make Callie Smalls move at double speed. At what seems like a snail's pace, she saunters over to the shrouded dress form on the right. Pausing at the perfect camera-ready angle she says, "Tonight's second favorite look belongs to ..."

Swoosh.

Holy crapballs. It's me.

"Michele. Duchess Maryn appreciated your use of color and styling, especially the shoes." Did I mention that I used fuchsia peep toe slingbacks that totally popped the color in the print lapel cape?

The cameras zoom in, and I try to control my facial expressions. I'm going for cool, calm, and collected. I'm pretty sure I portrayed bewildered, befuddled, and bedraggled. I'm hoping I'm more photogenic than my history suggests.

"Her favorite aspect of the outfit was the blazer cape, for both the uniqueness and construction. Well done."

I think people are congratulating me, but I can't move. I can't believe it. It's taking everything I have not to jump up and down and do a victory dance. I was the second favorite look in the very first episode! My instincts not to go with the black and magenta were spot on.

But whose look did she like better than mine? Who's my competition? As long as it's not Fink, I think I'll be okay. I think.

With the two runner-up dress forms flanking the sides, Callie takes position in the middle. "And now, Duchess Maryn will debut her favorite look of the night. Following this, she and Prince Stephan will make their public debut for the people of the United Republic of Montabago."

Something about what she says is making me think, but I can't identify what it's about because there's too much tension, too much anticipation waiting to see not only the winning look but what the duchess actually looks like.

"Without further ado, I introduce to you Duchess Maryn Medrovovich wearing a design by ..."

Seriously, I hate the dramatic pause. We don't

even have the canned music to make it more dramatic. It's lots of uncomfortable silence.

"Asher!"

With that, the mirrors part and enter Duchess Maryn. She looks stunning in Asher's dress. It's even better than it was on the model. It fits her well, is flattering, and stylish, without being too conservative.

Maryn looks a bit nervous. Her facial expressions, frankly, reflect the same anxiety and uncertainty us contestants have sported for the last few hours. I try to really look at her, to burn into my memory what she looks like and the nuances of her character for help in designing. I'll bet the others are doing the same. Glancing around, I'm distracted by Asher. He's beaming, and boy, is that man beautiful when he smiles. I'm pretty sure my mouth falls open, and I have to stop myself from drooling.

Yup, I've got it bad.

And then Callie Smalls is talking again, and I've missed my chance to analyze the way the duchess moves. Damn ADHD.

"So, Duchess, can you tell us why you chose this piece?"

She's standing there, twisting her fingers together. A sure sign she's as nervous as we are. Interesting. Her voice is deeper than I expected for someone her size. She's poised and well-spoken. "The construction of this garment is flawless. It was different yet conservative all at the same time."

"Do you have any critique for the designer?"

Maryn turns toward us, her eyes seeking out Asher. The large spotlight helps her find him. "I love this garment and cannot wait to see what else you have to offer. I do encourage you to be a bit more forward thinking with your styling though."

Called it.

Asher nods, as he's not given the opportunity to reply.

Callie Smalls again takes over. "That's it for this inaugural episode of *Made for Me*. Tune in to Bandwidth News Channel to see Forrest Tryken's interview with Prince Stephan and Duchess Maryn, as they make their official debut as a royal couple, announcing their engagement."

That's what I was thinking about before I got distracted. Well, one of the times I got distracted. So this show is airing almost in live time. I'm sure there's some production that's got to be done, but it's not going to air four months after we tape. I wonder what the delay is. I wonder how this will all work.

The cameras cut and the lights dim. We all sit in silence for a minute while the duchess, Taliance Ho, and Callie Smalls exit. No fraternizing with the designers I see. One of the producers tells us we're heading back to our apartments, and that the next assignment will start tomorrow.

Everyone's crowding around Asher, congratulating him. If it couldn't be me who won, then I'm glad it was him, at least in this first round. I really did love his dress.

We're ushered out into the waiting room. Lexington is whooping and hollering, while Sancere is unusually quiet. Her face has melted off.

"Here girl, fix your face a bit. You don't know if there'll be cameras back at the apartment." I hand her my makeup bag. She looks at me blankly. I stand on my tiptoes to whisper, "Your mascara is a mess and you're losing some eyelashes."

Her hands fly to her face and that panicked look is back. "Look, your dress was great. She obviously liked it. We didn't know about her trying them on. Now you know, and you can knock our socks off next time. You made it through, and that's all that matters."

She still doesn't say anything, but nods and then pulls me into a crushing hug.

"I've got my own makeup. The heavy duty kind. Thanks for looking out for me, Vanilla." With that, she takes off, presumably for the bathroom.

Great. Fink's nickname has stuck. If her mascara ever runs, I'll never tell her.

I'm crushed in another hug, but this time it's Asher. "Oh my God, we did it!" He even spins me around a little, like there's nothing to me.

He sort of takes my breath away, and not just because he's totally restricted all my air flow. When he puts me down, I say, "Congratulations. Your look was absolutely beautiful. I'd wear it in a heartbeat."

Against the din in the room, his breath hot against my neck, he whispers, "I was thinking about you when I designed it. What would look good on you." Then he breaks away as someone else starts to talk to him.

Huh.

Before I know it, the PAs are herding us into the elevators and down to the lobby. Walking right behind Lauren—I think her name is—I start to ask her what the plans are for the rest of the day when she stops dead. I stop too, not knowing why or what she's doing. Well, to be honest, I more trip over her than stop.

Of course I do, because across the lobby, waving enthusiastically at me, is Lincoln. This trip is nothing compared to the Little Joey drop. Or when I accidentally tackled him in this very lobby. But still, destined to be a klutz.

I can see Lincoln's grin from here. It's only been about three days (or is it two? Time is all warped right now) since I've seen him, but suddenly I'm homesick. I wave back, mirroring his enthusiasm.

That is, until I realize that Lauren is waving too. He's not waving at me. He's waving at her. I am such a doofus.

So now I have to pretend I wasn't waving at someone who was waving at someone else, and I do the 'run the hand through the hair' maneuver that fools exactly no one.

Lincoln's making his way over here. "Hey Lauren. Oh, hey Michele!" And with that, he hugs me. "How are you? How's it going?"

Lauren gives me a look. It's not a kind one. I don't care. "I'm still here, which is probably about all I can say."

Lauren interjects. "This is funny. How do you two know each other?"

Before I can say anything, Lincoln answers. "I've known Michele my whole life."

"That's right," I jump in. "Lincoln's best friends with my little cousin. He's practically part of the family. Like a cousin to me. An annoying little cousin."

"Aww, c'mon. You didn't think I was annoying when you were staying with me."

"Watching hours upon hours of *American Pickers* is annoying, but my mother raised me to be polite."

Simply mentioning my mom makes me homesick again.

"Speaking of which, any message you want me to give?"

Lauren gives me a death glare. Great. Another good friend. I excel at making them apparently. "Michele is not allowed to speak to anyone without specific production approval."

"Okay, I won't get you in trouble." Lincoln gives me another hug and a kiss on the cheek. "Don't drink too much in the off hours—producers love that footage. And knock 'em dead."

I can't help but smile as he turns and walks away. Lauren is fuming. I can practically feel the steam rising off her. I hope she doesn't have too much to do with post-production. If she does, I'm going to look horrible.

The rest of the group has stopped to wait for us in the lobby, so we hurry to catch up. Once we're piled into the shuttle, the questions start.

"Who was *that*?"

"I need to get me one of those."

"Damn girl, I didn't think you had that in you."

"Geez, Vanilla, he's more spicy than I would have pegged you for." Rat Fink is not winning any points with me. She glares at me again. "So he works here? Is that how you got in?"

I'm not even going to dignify that with a response.

Asher is uncharacteristically silent. He's watching the conversation like a tennis match. I'm watching him, watching the others fawn over me. Interesting. It only lasts a minute, then his performance face is on, and he makes some outrageous comment to Lexington that shifts the focus to him and gets the entire van hooting and hollering.

That whole episode took about fifteen seconds. But it was an important fifteen seconds. In that time I think I may have figured out two things: Asher is jealous of Lincoln; and he doesn't like not being the center of attention. One of those things could be good, but the other is probably very, very bad.

Chapter 14

An almost victory will only get you so far in one of these competitions. Every day, there's a new assignment. Every day you have to come up with a fantastic, innovative creation, and then make it. That's one of the things I like about sewing; taking something two-dimensional and making a three-dimensional, functional thing out of it.

But I don't like the pressure.

And I'm not sure how I feel about the spotlight either.

I mean, a little attention is good.

However, I did not like that look on Asher's face in the shuttle. It was like I disappointed him. Which is crazy. I mean, obviously I have a life outside of this show.

Well, not really. Not a real one anymore. Living in my parents' house, unemployed, boyfriend-less. Not much to say for almost thirty years on this earth.

Nevertheless, I feel the need to defend myself. "Lincoln's a family friend. He's my little cousin Tony's best friend. They're like my little brothers. I've known him since he was in diapers." I almost add that I used to call him 'Stinkbomb Lincoln' but I stop. It seems disrespectful to share that now. The cameras aren't rolling, but we're all still mic'd, so who knows what is being recorded. "I have a very big family, and he's just part of it."

Sancere nudges me with her hip. "That's too bad. Well, too bad for you, but I'll pay you to give him my number."

"Um, sure. I'll see if he's looking."

The conversation, thank goodness, finally turns back to the competition. Gordon isn't on the bus with us. But, from watching my fair share of reality TV, I know that he's still around. They'll keep us all around in some holding area so that no one knows in what order we're eliminated.

I bet the accommodations aren't as nice. What if they are though? What if they're as cushy and the food is as plentiful? I mean, it's not like they can starve us just because we're total failures as designers, right?

By the time we get back to the apartment, I've worked myself into an internal frenzy. I'm pretty good at that sort of thing. I kind of want a glass of wine to calm myself down, but I'm trying to be careful. It's way too early in the competition to lose control. And I know I can't be trusted around wine and Asher. Plus, I want to know everyone else's take on today. How the duchess looked, what her style might be, all the gory details.

Everyone is too keyed up. The voices are loud and I have a headache. My mom has always been a big believer that the primary cause of headaches is dehydration, and I'd be lying if I didn't sort of buy into her theory. I get a large glass of ice water, and rather than help analyze Duchess Maryn, I retire to my room. Kira's still out in the common area when I fall asleep.

I dream about fabric that is too slippery to pin and keeps sliding away before I can get it under the needle on the machine. Barrett, the royal jerk, is there, laughing at me. Asher keeps whispering in my ear, his breath hot on my skin. Lincoln and Tony are standing in the corner, watching.

I wake up in a cold sweat and look at the clock. I'm due to get up in about ten minutes anyway. Might as well head to the shower.

My hair hangs down in my face, and I start to examine it for split ends. I probably should have gotten a trim before I—WHAM. With my hair forming a curtain over my eyes, I can't see initially who, or what, I've run into.

"Oh, thank God it's you!" Lexington grabs my arms and pulls me into the bathroom. "I need your help!"

My feet aren't really working so well, and of course I'm still half asleep, so I stumble a little further. I'm so smooth.

"What the—what is going on?" Have I also mentioned that I'm quite gifted with the words?

"Michele, you've got to help me!" Lexington is looking pretty upset. Normally he's so calm and collected. "You know how the producers gave us the big talk about keeping the place in good shape?"

I nod, recalling the sit down we had about how we needed to not trash the apartments, as some other contestants on reality shows have been known to do. If we do, we are personally liable for any damage caused. I can only imagine what it would cost to fix things up in this neighborhood.

"Look!" He points to the wall next to the toilet. There's a hole in the wall. I'm almost positive it wasn't there last night.

"Did you do that?" I look at Lexington, whose brow is creased. He's biting his lower lip.

"How much do you think the producers will fine me? I don't have a lot of money."

"How did you even do it?"

Lexington squats down to examine the hole and then sinks onto the floor. "Oh, this is terrible. Maybe they won't notice it."

I bend over to look at it. It's about the size of a cantaloupe. "Yeah, there's no way they're not noticing it. What happened?"

"I don't want to say." He buries his face in his hands. Closing the lid on the toilet, I sit to wait. Let's face it, I still have to go, so standing around isn't going to be pleasant.

Just then, Asher walks in. "What—what are you doing in here?"

"Ssssh! Close the door!" Lexington motions frantically, as if his hand flapping will cause the door to shut.

Asher jumps in and closes the door, locking it behind him. "What are you two up to?"

"Lex here was just going to tell me how he put a massive hole in the wall, so we can figure out a way to keep him from having to pay for it."

Lexington looks at me. "How is me telling you how it happened going to help you come up with a solution?"

"It's not, but I need to hear how you did this."

Asher sits on the edge of the tub. "I think I need to hear this as well."

Lexington is flustered. He's pacing the bathroom, which is large by Midtown standards, but with three people in it, there's not a lot of room for pacing. Asher squats down to look at it. I stoop down, leaning over his shoulder. It's a big hole.

"It's a big hole." I feel very helpful, stating the obvious. I'm good like that.

"I can't afford this!" Lexington's voice is getting abnormally high and shrieky. "Plus, I don't want the producers to look at me badly. What if they think I'm irresponsible, and eliminate me?"

Asher stands, knocking me backwards a step or two. Lexington is pacing forward, and I'm sort of sandwiched in between them. I'm sure lots of girls would dream about this, but I'm back to thinking neither of them would look at me twice.

"Calm down, Lexington! You're going to wake the whole house." Asher reaches to Lexington, sort of ignoring me in between them. It's a super awkward group hug. "But you need to tell us what happened."

"After you stop smushing me." I'm not sure they can understand, as my face is pressed into Asher's chest. Not that I'm complaining.

I get the distinct impression that neither Asher nor Lexington is really aware of my presence, as Lexington leans his chin on my shoulder to be closer to Asher. "It's totally—I can't even!"

"Well, you need to even. We can't stay in here all morning. People will be trying to get in soon." The two of them continue talking as if I'm not in the middle. Awesome.

"Oh, gosh, it's just so ... well, I ..." Lexington breaks off. I think he may be on the verge of tears. Or hysterics. Or crushing my spine.

"Can't ... breathe ... here ..." I mean, I know I'm diminutive in stature, but this is ridiculous.

Lexington lets up finally and I almost collapse. Air feels good in my lungs again. I step aside and sit down on the edge of the tub. Asher follows me and Lexington sits back down on the closed toilet. "I was sitting here, you know ..." He gives a dramatic pause, elevating his eyebrows so that there's no doubt as to what he was doing. Ewww.

"And I realized I needed more, um, paper. But it's no big deal, because there's a big package."

True story. There is a Costco-sized package of toilet paper that sits in between the toilet and the wall. The space is only about eighteen inches wide, so I don't know what else you'd put there besides a large package of toilet paper.

"Anyway, it was brand new. I pulled open the packaging without an issue. But then, they're like wrapped inside. Like in groups of four or whatever. And, at the angle I was sitting at" —Lexington holds his hands, re-enacting the event—"I couldn't get a good grip on the inner packaging. And so I pulled but it didn't really budge. I pulled harder, knocked myself off balance, and as the plastic gave way, I fell and put my elbow through the wall."

Yup, that about explains the size and location of the hole.

The laughter that bursts forth from Asher startles me as it ricochets off the tile walls. "Oh Lex, that's priceless."

Lexington is on the verge of tears. Well, not really the verge, as I see them welling in his dark brown eyes, threatening to spill. "It's not funny."

Before I can help myself, a giggle sneaks out. I try to cover my mouth to keep it in, but it's useless. "You put a hole in the wall pooing."

Asher apparently finds this even funnier, and his laughter increases. I try to muffle him by putting my hand over his mouth and end up knocking us both into the tub.

In case there was any question, that hurts.

It also causes a commotion, as I flop around the tub, mostly on top of Asher, like a trout on the deck of a boat.

"Sssshhh! Someone's going to hear us!" Lexington's off the toilet and waving his arms about like a frantic chicken.

"This isn't how I pictured us together in a bathtub, you know." Asher's breath is hot on my neck and gives me pause.

Well, hello. He's been thinking about us in a bathtub?

I wish I had more time to think about this, but I don't, because there's a loud knock on the door.

"What's going on in there?" It's Katy, the head producer.

Well, crap.

Chapter 15

I try to ignore the whispers and the gossip while we're all getting ready and being transported to the studios. I know there's a lot of speculation about the events of this morning. Katy was relatively understanding, probably because Lexington was practically hysterical.

It didn't help that Asher and I were also in a similar state, frenzied with laughter. I mean, come on, this stuff is funny. Katy was going to take the situation to her bosses but thought it would be okay. Accidents happen.

By the time the shuttles pulled up to the studios, I realized that most of our fellow contestants didn't think it was an accident. Their dirty looks confirm any suspicion. I swear Fink could freeze boiling water with her glare. Even Breckyn and Weyler are abnormally icy. I pull Kira aside as we're walking into the building.

"Um, what's going on? Why am I getting the death glares from everyone?"

We're almost to the elevators, so we don't have much time.

"Because of your early morning escapades."

"Escapades? What do you mean?"

"The threesome in the bathroom."

The elevator door seals all of us in, plus some crew. It's tight to say the least, and I start to have some sympathies for sardines.

Threesome in the bathroom? What could she mean by that? She can't be talking about an actual— you know. I mean, other than Kira, I am closest with Asher and Lex. And we were the top three finishers in the first contest. I wonder if people are thinking we have an alliance or something like that. I bet that's it. They're thinking that we're going to band together and help each other out to get ahead.

Well, as much as I like Lexington and Asher (and I'm *still* pondering that bathtub comment he made), I'm in it to win it. For me. Not with some stupid alliance. I mean, this isn't *Survivor*. There's no way to get ahead by having secret agreements or crap like that. It's about hard work, talent, and ingenuity. I think I have those, and I plan to use them.

By the time the elevator doors part, I've shimmied up my bravado and am ready to take on whatever this assignment is.

Of course, that's before my heel catches in the tracks for the door, resulting in a face plant.

Really? Do I need more embarrassment? At least the cameras aren't—shoot. The crew was there, already filming.

Awesome.

I jump up before anyone can help me, smoothing my dress down. I'm pretty sure the whole elevator got a glimpse of my underwear. What is it with me and showing people my knickers? Why am I saying knickers? I've been hanging out with Asher too much.

And my shoe is broken too, the heel snapped right off. Fantastic. I pull the other shoe off and stuff them both in my bag. Maybe when I get home I can get this one fixed. Let's face it—I'm too broke to replace the shoes right now. My go-to nude patent leathers too. Figures.

I don't have time to stop and worry about it, as we're being hustled into the studio for the introduction and presentation. As we're waiting for Callie Smalls to come in, I start to worry about my feet. I hadn't thought about it, but we're most likely going shopping today. And I'm in bare foot. I only have my polka-dot stilettos and black ballet flats. I'd planned most of my outfits around the nude patents. Crapola. I wish there was a way to get another pair of shoes sent from home. For now, I'd settle for any pair of shoes at all. As the crew is setting up, adjusting mics and lights and cables, I wave furiously, trying to catch someone's—anyone's—attention.

Lauren, the crew member who seemed to get upset with me for knowing Lincoln, looks my way and then turns around again, totally ignoring me. We've strict orders to stay seated once our mics are on, so I'm trying not to get into too much trouble. Of course, I was the first one mic'd and most of the cast is still milling around. My luck is totally rolling today.

Lauren's rebuffing me does suggest that Lexington might not be wrong worrying that his destruction in the bathroom would get him kicked off the show. Has the word spread? Do they think I had something to do with it? Are Asher, Lexington, and I marked for elimination?

Finally, Katy notices my frantic waving. "Yes, Michele? Please do not tell me you have to go to the bathroom. You're supposed to go before we hook you up."

"No, it's not that. I, um, broke my shoe on the way in, and now I don't have anything to wear. Is there any way someone can run back to the apartment and get another pair of shoes?" I wiggle my bare toes at her. In addition to going shopping, being in the work room while barefoot would be treacherous too. Lots of pins get dropped on the floor.

"Jeezul Petes. Can't you people do anything right?"

I see I've made another fan.

Katy sighs. "We can't send anyone back right now, but I'll see what I can do. What size do you wear?"

"Six."

"Fine." Without more than that, Katy hustles away. I look around and notice Lauren still glaring at me. What the heck is her problem?

I don't have too much time to worry about it, as Callie Smalls makes her grand entrance. She's in a dress so short and tight it would be indecent on me. And she's about a foot taller than I am. She's built much like Christine. What I wouldn't give to have a figure like theirs ...

Before I can start waxing poetic about either my best friend or my short stature, Callie commands our attention.

"Some of you may be wondering how the timing on this show works."

Honestly, I'd never thought about it. I probably should have. I need to pay more attention to the important details, especially if I want to get ahead in this contest. I wonder what skin products Callie uses. She's probably close to forty, and I swear her skin is more luminous than mine. Oh, crap. I'm supposed to be paying attention.

"The episodes will air approximately one week apart. Duchess Maryn will appear in the winning outfit after each show has aired. This will allow the duchess time to travel back and forth to the United Republic of Montabago to make her necessary appearances and fulfill her duties and obligations. There will be five rounds of eliminations before the final round."

You know, this information would have been helpful to have before we started. Wait—five rounds before the final. There were ten of us. One elimination's already been done. We're down to nine contestants and four rounds. How many are they taking to the final?

Callie's still talking. Shoot, I really need to listen. "With that schedule, the final contestants—" Did she say how many and I missed it?" —will have approximately three weeks to prepare for the final assignment." There's murmuring amongst the contestants. "But, before you go thinking you know how the end will go, you don't. Be prepared for anything. And I mean *anything* to come up." Callie looks to the director, who gives her a nod. "All right then, I think we're ready to begin."

Katy sneaks over and hands me a pair of nude wedges. "They might be a tad big, but it's what I could find on set."

Before I can even really thank her, she's darted off. I catch Lauren still giving me the stink eye. Oh well. At least I'm not barefoot.

There's some more shuffling with the lighting and sound equipment, which gives me a moment to focus on what Callie said. Episodes will air weekly. They take us about three days to accomplish in real life. That means two assignments a week. Three weeks. But it'll take six to get to the finale. Obviously we all know about the wedding gown. I wonder how they're going to surprise us. What assignment will they throw at us? Will we have to scavenge for material to use? Will we be forced to use non-cloth, like CD's and garbage bags? Oh dear Lord, I feel faint at the thought.

I've got to get back to the math of it all. Unless it was figuring out how many yards of fabric I needed, or how to convert seam allowances, I've never been good at math. Nine contestants, four eliminations before the final. This feels like one of those word problems from school. And I can't even call Christine to help me through. No, I can do it. I passed all my high school math, even if it was just barely. I can figure this out. Figuring if three people make it to the final round, that leaves six people to be eliminated in four trials. Heck, I even *sound* like one of those math problems. So, they'll have to have at least one double elimination, but most likely two.

I sit up a little straighter, proud that I figured that out. Take that, Ms. Vertucci, who said I was bad at math and that I'd never accomplish anything. I don't have too much time to revel, because apparently the sound and lighting issues have been remedied and we're ready to go.

Assignment number two, let's do it.

Chapter 16

I'm totally at a loss. Assignment number two is a "casual day outfit." How casual is casual? Is it a yoga pants thing? Is it like a denim thing? Is there a royal protocol? We've only thirty minutes to design before we go shopping, and I'm still staring at a blank page. Again.

I've got nothing. I wish I could get onto Pinterest. Of course that would be about a four-hour time suck. I swear, it's like a dark hole. Maybe it's a good thing I don't have access to that.

And then it's time to go shop. Great. I guess I don't have to worry at all about the timeline. I'm going to be eliminated today, seeing as how I don't think nude is what they mean by casual.

Once again, I rely on the fabric to be my inspiration. And it doesn't let me down. I find a beautiful ivory rayon-poly that's got an incredible flow and drape, but will still hold a shape. And like the movement of the fabric, the ideas start flowing. The duchess is getting herself a jumpsuit. Most people my—our—height can never even consider a jumpsuit. Something about cutting a foot of fabric off the pants, and then the top doesn't fit the right way and the waist is too low—well, it never works. But it will when it's custom made to her proportions.

She's going to look fierce. And fashion forward, which is not my usual thing. Crap. I don't have time to second-guess myself. How will I make her über-trendy jumpsuit relevant retro?

Think. Think. Think.

Gah, there's not time to think. I grab whatever I can get my hands on and head to the cutting station, as we've been given the five-minute warning. Nuts, where did the time go? I guess that's why it helps to plan it all out before you get here.

I spend every penny and I'm not even sure what I have. The bag reveals buttons. I grabbed a handful of those. I'll have to work them in somehow. And I picked up some camel colored denim as well. And coral lining. What was I thinking? I'm not even sure how I knew what I was getting, but it's perfect. It's like the conscious part of my brain shut off while the creative part took over. I can see the entire outfit in my mind.

There's no time to waste. While everyone is laying out fabric and draping and cutting, I'm still sketching. A culotte-type pant. It will be critical to get the width and length absolutely right, otherwise she'll look short and squat. The waist will look like a pant waist, giving her shape and definition. Originally, I'd thought about doing a cami-style top, but based on her bust size, opted for a tank style that she can wear a normal bra with. I'm adding a triangle cut-out detail to the back that exposes skin, but is still modest. Secret sexiness that can be hidden with the jacket.

As for the jacket, here's where my usual style is going to come in a bit. The denim gives it a more casual feel, but I'm designing the heck out of it. It's more of a cape with a large, standing cowl neck. The neck wraps across and a large button secures one side to the other, over on the left side. The sleeves are three-quarter and match the proportions of the pants, while the back looks like a cape. The length of the jacket-cape is the same as that of the end of the sleeves, creating a visual line. The coral lining peeks through from the front. I may even edge the pockets on the jumpsuit with the coral. I know, I said no more handmade piping, but when inspiration talks, you listen.

Before I know it, I'm being called to go on my dinner break. It's after six p.m. Holy cow! Where did the day go? The stiffness in my back and neck certainly indicate that I've been bent over my table all day. I haven't even had time to look around. I try to get a glimpse of what the others are working on as I leave the room.

Tonight, I'm with Butch. He doesn't have anything to say to me. I'm getting the glares from him as well. Okey-dokey. I've probably not shared more than ten words directly with Butch since I've been here. I try again, only to be met with stony silence. Message received.

We're mandated to take a thirty-minute break, but I'm done eating after about ten minutes. I only want to get back to my project. I'd initially thought of doing a waistband to look like a pants waist, complete with faux button and all, but that won't work with the one-piece jumpsuit. I'm going to have to put a drawstring in so she can make the garment large enough to step into. I'd been torn over whether to do a side zipper or back, and finally went with the back, working it into the cut-out detail.

Finally dinner is over and I'm back to my table. I'm so lost in my work that I'm startled when Lexington, prompted by Katy, calls time for the night. Eleven o'clock! Only the feeling of sand in my eyes and heaviness in my limbs tells me that the night has flown by, and it is indeed that late.

All I want is my bed. We've still got the shuttle ride back. As soon as I sit down, fatigue engulfs me, and I can barely keep my eyes open. Asher wiggles in next to me, elbowing me a bit.

"Tired?"

I let out a large yawn. "I could go to sleep right now."

He shrugs his shoulder at me. "Go ahead. I'll wake you when we get there."

I'm too tired to argue, and I let myself drift off. The cast is somewhat more subdued than in previous shuttle rides. I guess I'm not the only one who's this tired.

The stopping of the shuttle jostles me awake. Dear heavens, I hope I didn't drool on Asher. We're all like walking zombies. Once in the apartment, I know I'm forgoing the socialization. It seems everyone's mad at me anyway, though no one seems to be giving Asher and Lexington the silent treatment. Why would they only be mad at me? Doesn't make sense. I grab a bottle of water and head right to bed, not even stopping to wash my face.

Naturally, the moment I'm tucked in bed, my mind starts whirling. Not only about my design, but about the silent treatment I seem to be getting. Why? What did I do? What was it Kira had said about the alliance between Asher, Lexington, and me? She's not in the room yet. I need to ask her. If she's talking to me that is.

I don't have to wait long before Kira finally retires. I'm glad to know I'm not the only one fatigue is affecting. Kira's got a book out and is obviously planning on reading for a while. Here goes nothing.

"Hey, can I ask you something?" I don't wait for her to answer. "Why is everyone giving me the cold shoulder? What did I do?"

She puts her book down and looks at me. "I told you—everyone's upset about the threesome."

"Right, but they're only mad at me. Not Lex or Ash."

"That's how things are." She shrugs. "Stupid double standard."

"I don't understand why though—there's no way that it really impacts anything."

"No, I don't suppose it does, but you know how catty people can get. Especially when jealousy rears its ugly head."

"What is there to be jealous of?" This does not make sense to me. "It's not like I can use my friendship with Lexington and Asher to get further in the competition. We're all judged on our own work."

"It has nothing to do with the competition." Kira picks up her book again. She sounds exasperated.

"Why wouldn't it?" I'm thoroughly confused.

"Are you dense? Why would it? You three getting freaky in the bathroom *obviously* has nothing to do with your sewing skills. It's just that Asher and Lexington are the best looking, most eligible men here, and you took both of them, which is pissing off the girls and the boys. Butch is still trying to figure out how you managed to get Lexington."

Wait—what?

I think my eyes must be as wide as dinner plates. My mouth is most certainly hanging open.

Kira takes one look at me and bursts out laughing. "Oh God, Fink is right. You really are vanilla!"

That's enough to shut my mouth and look down. I know my face shows a look of hurt. A poker face is not a strength of mine.

Kira sits up rapidly and swings her feet to the floor. "No, Michele, I don't mean that in a bad way. It's just, well, you're a bit naive. What did you think I meant when I said threesome?"

I look at my hands, clasped in my lap. I'm sitting up in bed, my legs stretched in front of me. I certainly can't look at Kira now. "I thought you meant that we were forming an alliance or something like that to get a competition advantage."

"Oh, well, I could see that. But no, that's not what I meant."

"So you literally meant—" I can't get the words out.

"Yeah, that you were getting freaky in the bathroom with two fine men. And that you had such a good time doing it, one of you broke the wall. We've been trying to figure out all day who it was and what body part."

It does make me smile, a tiny bit. How do I tell her that such a thing never crossed my mind? "I wish it were as exciting as all that. Sometime before I got up, Lexington fell off the toilet and through the wall trying to get a roll of toilet paper out of the package. He started freaking out, thinking that the producers would not only fine him but eliminate him for destruction of property. I simply happened to find him on my way to the bathroom."

"How'd Asher get involved?"

I shrug. "He just came in. Maybe he had to go too. I dunno. We got sidetracked. And I thought it was funny, and then I started laughing and fell into the bathtub."

"Is that what the ruckus was? We heard a lot."

Then it dawns on me. "So you all thought ..."

Kira laughs. "I was surprised you had it in you but was proud of you."

I'm sure my face is three shades of scarlet. I guess I am pretty vanilla, especially for this crowd. "I don't have it in me. Certainly not with everyone around too. Plus ..." I trail off, not even sure how to form the next sentences without sounding like a complete moron.

"Plus what?"

I have to take a deep breath before I can even start. "Well, it's pretty obvious that Lexington is gay, right? And I'm confused about Asher. Sometimes he's pretty into Lex—I mean, he did take Lexington into his arms to comfort him while we were in the bathroom." I leave out the part where I was sandwiched in between them. "But then, sometimes I think he's flirting with me. I don't get it."

"He's bi." Kira says it like it's the most obvious thing in the world. Well, duh. How did I not see that? Probably the same way I missed the torrid love affair between Trinity and Mr. Bayly that brought about the end of U'nique Boutique. And most definitely the way I missed that Barrett the rat was using me for sex and had an actual girlfriend on the side.

Apparently, I can be pretty dense when it comes to those around me.

"Well, that makes sense, I guess."

"Yeah, he's like the definition of the alpha male. Everyone's drawn to him."

"And he's drawn to everyone." I try to hide the glumness but don't think I do a very good job.

"Haven't you known any LGBT people? Where are you from again?"

"Of course I know gay people. I was in design school for a year. Well, almost a year. And I had a hairdresser who transitioned. It's just, well the bi thing confuses me. Like how do you know? How do they know? How can you trust him to be with anyone?"

"Aren't you putting the cart a little before the horse here? Didn't you say nothing happened in that bathroom?"

"Well, yeah, but he does make these comments that make me wonder. And look at him—I'd be stupid not to think he's hot."

"Too pretty boy."

This is about as personal as Kira and I've gotten. Now, despite the fatigue, I can't help but want to know more about her. I mean, she's obviously talented, but she—well, she certainly marches to her own drummer. Her green hair is growing out, and she's dyed the roots blue. It's pretty fantastic and more than I could ever imagine.

"My husband is a big dough-boy lumberjack type who rides a Harley and would bust a gut laughing at the primping and preening these pretty boys do."

"You're married? How old are you?"

"I'm thirty-five. What are you? Twenty-one?"

"Twenty-nine, actually."

"Oh."

Huh. I wonder what that is supposed to mean. "You thought I was twenty-one because I live with my parents and work in retail, except I'm out of work right now and have no viable prospects in my life?"

Kira throws her arms up. "Whoa—defensive much? I mean it's because you look young. Which, trust me, is a good thing."

"Oh, sorry. But yeah, I don't have my life together, which I'm hoping this show will help me do. I'm trying to get my Etsy business off the ground." I tell her about my plan, and she nods in agreement.

"So nobody special? From your confusion and reactions earlier, I'm gonna make the wild assumption that you date men?"

I fill her in on the Barrett the rat debacle, how my family is trying to set me up, how I've been having more fun hanging out with Tony and Lincoln than actually dating, and how I may or may not be having some impure thoughts about Asher.

"Is Lincoln the guy from the lobby? Who works here?"

I nod.

"He's some nice eye candy too, if you don't mind me saying."

"Lincoln?" I think about him for a minute. It's hard to picture Lincoln as he is now. I still see the kid

I grew up with. But I remember the night he drove me home, noticing how fine his jaw looked. And how his eyes look piercing blue sometimes. "But we're just friends. Like from when we were kids. That's not how I think of him, and certainly not how he thinks of me."

Chapter 17

The second round of eliminations are no easier than the first. I doubt they'll ever be any easier or that I'll get over the feeling of wanting to puke my guts out. Knowing me, it's a good possibility. The runway styles were varied, and I'm guessing I'm not the only one who struggled with what a casual day looks like for royalty. There was a wide variety—from jeans (Breckyn) to a maxi dress (Fink) and everything in between. Other than mine, which I obviously liked the best, Asher's again was fantastic. Sancere's dress was gorgeous, and I'll bet my butt it has a working zipper this time.

Like last time, the rack comes out first. Like last time, Breckyn's on it. That doesn't bode well for her. Butch's leather pants also make the rack, as does Lexington's dress. It, like Breckyn's in the first round, has nothing really wrong with it—it's just boring. I glance at Lexington. He's fuming.

Crap. I wonder if he thinks the bathroom incident has something to do with it. His dress is okay, but not for this kind of high-stakes game. At least he's not called up for being in the bottom two. I subliminally imagine Fink being on the rack, but that's probably because I hate her. Two weeks on the rack is apparently the kiss of death and Breckyn is sent home. Fink is still standing up with Callie, and if I thought she had a heart, I would say she's too scared to move and sit back down. I know Lexington is relieved, but he's still obviously upset. I would be too.

I'm more prepared now for how long this day takes, but it doesn't make it any easier. Especially since I'm still getting the cold shoulder from the majority of the cast. The down time is agonizingly long when you're on your own.

We're in the back room, waiting for the winners to be revealed, when Asher plops down next to me, handing me a bottle of water.

"You look like you need this."

"I need something stronger. Something to warm up the environment."

"What do you mean? Are you cold? Do you need someone to warm you up?" He looks me up and down, and I break out in goose bumps. Not the cold kind.

"No, it's that no one except for you and Kira is speaking to me. Everyone thinks that you, Lexington, and I had a threesome in the bathroom."

Asher's laughter is loud, causing everyone to look at us. He's casually draped on the couch, one arm behind me, one ankle crossed over the other knee. Nothing seems to bother him. "Well, I can only wish that's what had been going on. You know Lex is convinced that he's on the rack because of the bathroom."

"I was thinking that, from the look on his face."

"Who do you think are top three?"

I blush a little and look at my feet. "I want to say you, me, and Sancere. I really liked her dress."

Asher nods. "I bet you're in the top again. That jumpsuit was killer and the cape was fierce. She'd be a fool not to pick it."

"Yeah, but when they said her day event is a trip to a day care, I knew I blew it."

"Why?" His brow furrows. I could fall into those green eyes forever.

"White and little kids don't go well together."

"If the producers of *Jurassic World* thought it was okay for Bryce Dallas Howard to wear white, then a photo op at a day care should be no big deal."

"Do we really think she could out run a T-rex, let alone in stilettos? I mean, why didn't she kick them off at some point? Absolutely ridiculous. That movie is so unbelievable."

"Right, because the whole dinosaur thing is plausible."

I'm such an idiot. "Well, other than that, I guess. I mean, that is the whole plot. You have to suspend disbelief somewhere."

"Well, if it's good enough for *Jurassic World*, I'm sure the duchess can make due." His arm, which had been resting on the back of the couch, sneaks down to give my shoulder a squeeze. But then he's up and across the room to talk to Weyler.

She's flirting with him. What the heck? I get put on ice because they think I fooled around with Asher, but it's okay that he fooled around with me. I fold my arms across my chest in a huff. Stupid double standard.

The day is taking forever, but at least this time I know that they're setting up the dress forms and Duchess Maryn is donning one of our outfits. Still, it's going way too slow. You know, on reality shows when they do the big dramatic pauses and then it goes to commercial, and it about drives you nuts? Yeah, well in real life it takes about a million times longer and is gut-wrenchingly agonizing. I'm sort of starting to feel that reality shows should be banned for cruel and unusual punishment. No wonder so many former contestants end up as train wrecks. I'm probably going to have serious psychological damage. And it's only round two.

The blue chairs in the presentation room may look nice, but they're not comfortable. Heck, I don't think I'd be comfortable in anything right now, my nerves are wound so tight. The lines around Asher's mouth indicate he's feeling the same way, although I think he's doing a better job at not letting it show.

Have I mentioned that I'm a complete and total buffoon when it comes to my one-on-one interviews? Yup. They haven't gotten any better. I either sit around with my mouth agape, waiting for something to fly in, or I'm yammering nonsensically. There's no gray area. I have got to be the worst contestant in the history of reality TV. I can't handle the pressure, I'm boring, and I freak out with every round.

I'm so busy on my downward spiral of self-doubt that I don't notice Callie unveiling the left mannequin. Which reveals Sancere's dress. I repeat myself. Holy crapballs. Could I really be top two? There is no way this can really be happening.

Could it really be Asher and me? Again? He glances over and gives me a wink.

And I'm going to have a hard time paying attention again because I'm distracted by Asher. Dang, he's cute.

No, must pay attention. Must not be distracted by the cute boy. Uh, man. Asher is definitely a man. Lincoln is a boy. Except he's not really anymore either. Why am I thinking this now? CRAP. I NEED TO FOCUS.

Callie is waltzing over to the right dress form. Doesn't she know how slow she's moving? C'mon, lady. You're killing me.

Her flourish reveals Asher's look. Oh my gosh, what if I'm right and we're the top three? That means I'm the winning look. I want to bite my fingernails, but movement of one of the cameras catches my eye. Instead, I shove my hands under my thighs, gripping the front edge of the chair until my fingers ache.

"And now for the duchess, wearing her favorite look from the casual day assignment ..." Callie steps to the side and out of the spotlight. The lights adjust to the top of the runway where Duchess Maryn makes her entrance.

In a beautiful ivory jumpsuit and camel cape-coat.

Holy crapballs. I won this assignment.

****

Before I can even change my clothes, the wine is flowing and, for once, I decide to partake. Based on how keyed up I am, without wine, sleep will never come. One glass.

Famous last words.

One bottle is more like it. Whose bright idea is it to provide an endless supply of liquor? Oh, the producers who want the juicy, gory drama.

I mean, it could have been so much worse, I suppose. The hangover I have is part of the problem, especially with the early, early wake-up call. Maybe the lack of sleep is why I feel so terrible. Yeah, that's it.

I'm sure it has nothing to do with how I pranced around and *literally* shoved Lexington out of the way so I could cozy up next to Asher. Well, on Asher's lap to be precise.

I do a face palm, but it only serves to make my headache worse.

I don't mean to groan out loud, but I do.

"Yes, it was that bad."

I sit up in bed, startled by my roommate's voice. "What?"

Kira is sitting at the edge of her bed, already dressed. "Yes, it was that bad. You were a total shameless flirt, almost bordering on hussy."

I've started to sit up but now flop back. "Uggh. Why did I drink?"

"I'm not gonna lie, it was pretty funny. Especially when you bullied your way between Ash and Lex."

"I thought I did that. Ugh. How bad—no, don't answer that. I'm never drinking again. Or looking at Ash."

"Oh, you'll look at him again."

"Why do you say that?"

"Considering he wanted to stay in here with you last night, I'd say it's not over."

"He what?" And then the pieces come sliding back into place. He *did* want to stay in here. And I told him no. Go me. Or not. I don't know. "Was there kissing?" I don't have to wait for her to answer. I *remember* the answer. Oh yeah. "Kira, did I do the right thing? Should I have let him in?"

"Well, considering I'm in here too, I'd say yes, you did the right thing not letting him in. Wait until one of your roommates is eliminated to shack up, will ya?"

"Who's to say that we wouldn't be eliminated before our roommates?"

Kira's up and moving about the room, picking up her clothes that are strewn on the end of the bed. "We were talking about it last night while you two were all lovey-dovey and whispering sweet nothings into each other's ears. You two are definitely the front-runners. And then watching the two of you together, it was like you are the power couple. On a related note, you should watch your back. Fink has it in for you. And Butch—he's got a vicious streak."

"Wow, that's a lot of information all at once." I try to process it. "And I already know they hate me. Ever since the threesome that wasn't. Anyone else I should watch out for?"

"Lex. Definitely Lex."

"Really? He's so funny and nice. He's the third musketeer."

"Yeah, but after last night, you're not his friend. You stole his man."

I can feel my brow furrowing. I need to ask her opinion but don't know how to phrase it.

"You're confused by the bi thing again, aren't you?"

"Is it that obvious?"

"You read like an open book. You should never, ever play poker."

"I already know that. So, if, like Asher and I were together, and Lex, you know, like hit on him, would he cheat on me with Lex?"

"You get that the only person who could answer that is Asher. And I'm guessing he'll tell you no, regardless of what the truth is."

"Yeah, that's what I'm afraid of. I've been down this road before. Well, not *this* road, obviously, but you know, with the louse who cheats on me."

I've done a pretty decent job not thinking about all that wasted time with Barrett the rat. And he didn't *technically* cheat on me, because there wasn't supposed to be an expectation of a relationship. Except, of course, I expected him to change.

But that's neither here nor there right now. Barrett the rat is nothing. The matter at hand is that I made a gigantic fool of myself last night.

Stupid wine.

Stupid me.

And I feel like pooh.

Fabulous.

Chapter 18

Luck, if you want to call it that, swings slightly in my direction. Attempting to be creative while nursing a large hangover is quite difficult. This is where the luck thing comes in. Instead of jumping right into the next assignment, we're having a "production day." It gives the editing crew time to catch up on what they have to do. We all have to do some sit-down interviews as well. The best part is we all get to call our families.

It's so weird. I've only been here a little over a week, I think. In all honesty, I've sort of lost track of time. Probably because our days are so long that one day seems like three and three days passes as quickly as one. I want to call my mom to see how she's feeling. She had a follow-up last—this?—week, and we're all hoping for a clean bill of health. Plus, Lynn was going to see a doctor for fertility stuff. That's sort of the sucky thing about being here—I'm missing out on my family's life.

On the other hand, I haven't been asked why I'm not married, or when I'm going to get a real job, or why I can't mange my money better. Yes, they all know the story. Secrets are not something that work in my family. It doesn't mean they don't try—everything starts with "I have to tell you something and you can't tell *anyone*." Yeah right. We can't reveal any details about the show, so this phone call will have to be guarded on my part. One little slip and it will spread through my family like wildfire.

It's not my turn for interviews or phone calls, so I'm hiding out in my room. Actually in my bed, covers over head and all. I'm super mature, I know. I don't want to see anyone, mostly Asher. I'm mortified by my behavior.

It's not like I'm a prude—far from it. Obviously, I've spent the last year in a "friends with benefits" relationship with Barrett the rat. I know it was stupid. Christine used to tell me that all the time. Mostly because she knows me better than I know myself. I wanted to think that I was capable of being in that sort of casual relationship. But I'm not. All along, even though I vehemently denied it, I was waiting for Barrett the rat to commit to me. To realize that I was worth more than a booty call. But, since I didn't act like I was worth more, why should he treat me that way?

Oh, good Lord, I sound like Aunt Maria. If you know what I mean.

When that realization hits me, my first instinct is to call Tony. He'd get a huge kick out of it. I can picture him and Lincoln busting a gut, comparing me to one of the old Italian biddies we've mocked our entire lives. But I can't call him because I only get one call home. Sort of like prison, but with more stylish uniforms.

I haul myself up and head down to the phone room. It's empty, so I sneak in and call my parents. Dad answers because, well, he always does. Even if he's in a sound sleep, he'll answer the phone. Of course, he won't remember that he talked to you. This resulted in many groundings for my brother John who would call to say he'd be late, and Dad wouldn't remember. Hopefully at this early hours, that won't happen.

But I didn't expect them not to answer. What day of the week is it? Where could they be? I'd call Mom's cell phone, but most of the time she either doesn't hear it or can't figure out how to answer. And it's not like she can call me back. I stare at the phone, somewhat defeated. This is not what I need today. I should call Lynn.

I'm a terrible person, but I don't want to. I don't want to talk to her until she has good news. It's too hard to hear the heartbreak in her voice every month, trying so hard to be cheerful. I know she's hurting, and I'd do anything to help, but it's hard when she lashes out and makes comments like, "At least you don't have your life together. I couldn't bear it if you beat me to having a child." I'm in no place to have a baby—*shudder*—but still, that's just mean. Needing to hear a friendly voice from home, I call Tony.

"Michele! How's it going? Are you still in? Can you tell me that?"

"You know I can't. I am super hungover right now, so I'd appreciate you not yelling though."

"Linc said he saw you the other day."

"Yeah, in the lobby. It was good to see a face from home."

"It's weird that you two are in the same building every day but don't see each other."

"There's a lot of people you don't see every day in a city of a billion."

"A billion?"

"Thirteen million. Whatever." I stick my tongue out at the phone, but it's not nearly as satisfying as having him see me do it. "Growing up, my mom only saw our next door neighbor when someone else we knew was in the hospital where she worked. Same sort of thing."

"Not at all, but you've always marched to your own drummer."

"That I have. And it's gotten me this far."

"Your parents' basement?"

This time, my unseen gesture is not as polite, and I would certainly get a scolding if my mom or aunts saw me do it.

"I don't live in the basement, I only work down there. I live in my childhood bedroom, for the record. But you know, this contest has sort of given me focus. No matter what the outcome, I know what I want to do now. And that's something, because I never knew before."

"I thought you always wanted to be a designer?"

"No, I always wanted to sew, and that's a whole lot different. I don't think I really thought I had it in me to be a designer. But now I know that I not only can design, but that I'm already there!"

"Michele, this is the first time I've heard you this excited about, like, actual work."

"Ha ha, very funny. But it's true. What's also true is that I feel like pooh, and if I don't go back to bed, I may puke. I have to be on camera in a bit, and me looking green and hungover is not how I want to do it."

We disconnect, and I slink back to my room, careful not to be seen by anyone. Aaaaah, my bed feels so good, even if I am in it by myself, and sleep descends.

One of the producers sticks his head in the room. I can't really tell who it is, since I'm still buried under the covers. "Fifteen minutes and you're due in the interview room."

Ugh. I'm guessing I look like hell. I know I feel like it. My stomach rolls and my head pounds as I get out of bed. No time for a shower. I say a quick prayer to Mary Magdalene, the patron saint of hairdressers, that I can do something with the rat's nest that is undoubtedly on my head.

I'm ready in fourteen minutes. It's probably a world record for me. I've managed a teased pony and some concealer hopefully helps with the bags under my eyes. That, and the hemorrhoid cream. Don't judge. It works.

Passing through the kitchen, I grab a can of soda and a bagel. FYI, chugging a can of densely carbonated soda with an upset stomach on the way to do an interview is not the smartest idea. The bubbles well up in my chest, burning and pressing until there is nothing I can do but belch. Like a big 'ole truck driver burp. On camera.

On one hand, I feel much better. On the other, the camera was rolling.

"Oh, no, no, NO! Please delete that! You can't use that. I drank a soda too quickly on my way in, and the carbonation got to me. Please don't use that!"

The camera man is laughing. The producer who called me in, Scott, looks mortified. I am a camera moron. Every time I get in front of the camera, I make a fool of myself. I don't even know why. It may be my destiny. I should probably look up the patron saint of "I'm a jackhole on camera" as soon as possible.

Crap, no internet access. I think my trend is destined to continue. There's gotta be someone I can pray to. If my mom knew how to look it up, I'd ask her when I get my next phone call, but considering she calls the computer the "e-mail machine," I don't think it's going to work. But I digress. Again.

The camera guy has composed himself, and I'm doing the best I can. Scott looks at me. "Are you ready now? No more scary noises?"

My face burns with the heat of embarrassment. "I think I'm okay now." I hope.

I don't know if he had his questions planned out ahead of time, or if he exacted revenge for my inadvertent gaseous emanations.

"You've finished number two and then number one in the first two assignments. Are you worried about peaking and burning out too early?"

No, but I am now. Thanks a lot.

"You look pretty tired. Are you drinking too much? Do you have a drinking problem?"

"No, not at all. I meant only to have one glass of wine last night, just to help me unwind after the judging ceremony. I was pretty excited, as would be expected."

"So you expected to win?"

"No, not at all. I mean I hoped I would, but doesn't everyone?"

"So, you're thinking that you're one of the stronger designers here?"

Red alert. Red alert. I smell a trap. I sit up a little straighter. "I think everyone here is very talented, otherwise we wouldn't be here. It's anyone's game."

He's on to me, that I'm on to him. A small smile spreads across his face. It makes him look like a cartoonish weasel. I've only ever seen a weasel once—it was frantically hopping across a road, so I didn't see its smile. But still, Scott looks as I imagine a smiling weasel would.

"Well, then, do you think engaging in romantic *engagements* is a wise strategy? Are you trying to distract Asher, who appears to be your biggest competition?"

There were no cameras rolling last night. At least I don't think there were. People have big mouths.

"I'm single, in my twenties—" I pause, thinking about the date, "—for another week at least. If I want to have some fun or be friendly with other people, why not?"

"Oh, you're not trying to use your sex appeal to foil the competition? Distract them, build a bond so you can get favors, and then use it to your advantage?"

My blood begins to boil, as I'm sure this is not the line of questioning Asher had to face. Stupid bloody double standards.

"I'm here to design and to win. I've got a company—New Michele Designs—that I'm trying to build. What happens off camera should stay off camera. And I think we're done here." Without waiting to be dismissed, I stand up and unclip my mic, and proceed to storm out.

Which would have gone so much better had I not tripped on a cable.

But whatever, I'm not going to sit there and be accused of selling myself or using sex to cheat my way to a win.

Chapter 19

The high of winning is quickly destroyed when I end up on the rack in the third round. Just goes to show you, this is really anyone's game. The assignment was to design an outfit for a charity function. My use of faux fur, even though it was as fake as a Gucci bag from a street vendor, was not appreciated. It would have been helpful if they'd told us that the charity event was for PETA.

At least Taliance Ho liked my design.

I should be grateful. In fact I am—very--because this was a double elimination round. Butch and Kira were not so lucky. I don't know if I'm sadder that I was on the rack or that Kira's going home.

Arriving back to the apartment, I only want to sit in our—my—room and reflect. Kira left me a lovely note with her contact information and promises to reach out on social media as soon as we're restored to the land of the internet.

Totally aside, do you know how hard it is to quit all social media and internet cold turkey? I feel like I should have had a twelve-step program or something.

Again I wonder what happens when you get eliminated. I say a quick prayer that I won't find out anytime soon. Being on the rack sucked. Especially when Fink had one of the top designs. Lexington won, and Asher was number two again. I could see him grit his teeth and grimace when his design was revealed. It does seem to get his goat that he's not number one.

Typical alpha.

I wonder if tonight he'll be all cozied up with Lexington. Maybe that's *his* strategy—distract the competition. Maybe I have been a bit sidetracked by Asher. But, that's in the off hours. When I'm in the workroom, I'm in my zone. I ended up on the rack today due to an unfortunate choice of fabric. That's it. They had no issues with design or construction. Now, if the duchess had been going to a benefit for the NRA, maybe I'd have won.

But that's neither here nor there. I know the wedding gown assignment will be coming up, and I've got to start thinking about it. How can I incorporate buttons on a wedding dress and still make it look elegant? Obviously, I can put the tiny buttons down the back, but I don't want to be obvious. Plus, corset bodices are very in right now, although I doubt Duchess Maryn would go for the risqué design of a corset.

I wish they'd tell us more about her; her likes and dislikes. Let us have a conversation with her or hang out for a while or something. She seems so reserved, sitting in her chair across the runway. Even when she makes her debut in the winning outfit she doesn't speak, not really. I'm not sure I've even heard her voice. Maybe she's spoken, but I don't remember it. In my head, she's got a British accent though. Maybe because I think all royalty should be British. I don't know what the native language of Montabago is. Or remember where it is. Or anything about it. It'd also be nice if they gave us a little background about the country. It might help in our designs. Or maybe it would help if I could recall the things I know I've looked up.

It's like they don't want us to succeed.

Flopping backward on my bed, I press the heels of my hands into my eyes, trying to focus on what I envision the duchess walking down the aisle in. I actually do manage to concentrate for a few minutes, which leads me to be startled when a weight depresses the mattress next to me.

"Hey, you okay?"

"Asher, what are you doing in here?" I try to sit up, but his arm is across my waist, making it hard for me to go anywhere.

"I came to check in on you. You seemed pretty upset today."

"Well, I was on the rack. You'd be upset too, if you were there." I sort of want to add, "Not that you'll ever be there."

"It was the unfortunate fur thing."

"But it was faux! And how were we supposed to know that it was a PETA thing?"

"I know." He's lying on his side, resting his head on his arm, outstretched up and over my head. The other arm is still casually draped across my abdomen. I feel his fingers start to stroke my hair. "Anyone could have made that mistake. But your design was killer."

I want to be glib. "Yeah, killer of faux fur. The stuffed animals of the world are outraged at my choice of fabric." Even making a joke doesn't help. I feel tears starting to form. Tears of loneliness. Of homesickness. Of want. Of frustration.

Asher moves his head so his mouth is next to my ear. "It's okay. Don't be upset. Shake it off and move on." He's still playing with my hair and is using his other hand to pull me closer. It would be so easy right now. I close my eyes for a minute, and he takes that as an opportunity to press his lips to mine. I let him. I don't just let him, I welcome him. Invite him into my space. He's maneuvered his way on top of me.

Well, this is good.

No, wait, no it's not. I like Asher, I do. He's smokin' hot and engaging. He certainly has a magnetic personality. But that's not why I'm here. For once in my life, I need to stay focused. With an internal strength I didn't know I had, I gently push Asher up a bit.

"Ash, wait."

He bends his head back down and starts kissing my neck. Ooooh, that's nice. No, wait, I don't want this to continue. Yes I do. No, even though I want it, I can't have it right now. I push him up again.

"Ash, stop." I push a little harder. I'm breathless. Dang, the man made me breathless. I wonder what else he could do. No, STOP. I can't wonder. "We can't do this right now."

He rolls off and places himself on the bed next to me, so we're shoulder to shoulder. "No, I suppose we can't."

"It's not that I don't ... want ... to," suddenly I'm stammering like an idiot. I'm so smooth. "Because I do. Well, I think maybe I do."

"You think maybe? That's a rousing endorsement."

"There's so much going on right now. You know, the contest, and everything."

He chuckles. "I get it. Like, we should be focused and stuff." He uses an American accent, and I can't help but wonder if he's mocking me.

"That's so eloquent. Focused and stuff."

"I never said I was good with words."

"That's funny, because usually you're pretty smooth." Now it's my turn to roll on my side to face him. He's staring at the ceiling as if it's riveting. "And you know you know it, so don't try that humble routine with me."

He laughs, turning his head toward mine. We're only inches apart again. I really wish I could kiss him again. I probably shouldn't though. So instead, I talk. "Tell me more about you. You have a menswear line? You said your partner wasn't supportive of this venture. What's going on with that?"

"Trig doesn't want to branch out into women's wear. He's happy with where the company is and wants to put all the company's resources back into the business." Have I mentioned how much I like listening to Asher speak? That lovely accent could make reading a grocery list sound sexy.

"And you have a differing opinion, I take it?"

"We're based out of L.A., and I'm tired of it. I don't like California. I'm looking to expand not only into women's fashion but into more of a European market. I'm thinking of going back to England."

"Oh, to be near your family?"

"Crikey no, nothing like that. I miss London. I moved there after uni. I'm done with the West Coast."

I wonder what his family's like and how it can be that he's so far away with no desire to return home. I mean, I get not wanting to be *in* your parents' home, but that's not what I mean.

"So this contest would be the perfect springboard to the European market for you."

"That's the plan."

I inch a bit away. As much as my loins may want to, this is a bad idea. One of us is bound to get hurt. After all, we can't both win.

Chapter 20

Assignment number four is what we've all been waiting for—the formal event. It's like the precursor to the wedding gown. Plus, making a gown is a whole lot harder than a regular dress. There's so much more to the construction.

I know what I want to do—well, I at least have an idea—before we head to the store. I find the ice blue matte satin that I want, knowing the contrast with Duchess Maryn's chestnut hair will be striking. The embellishments—the buttons—will be what makes this gown. We get two full days to work on our creations, and I need every single minute.

The gown has wide-set straps that sit right over the crest of the shoulders, creating a wide scoop neckline. It flatters the collar bone but doesn't reveal too much cleavage. Modest but stylish. It has a fitted bodice with an angled dropped waist that will provide the illusion of a long body. The skirt—that's the show stopper. Large voluminous folds ruffle down asymmetrically from the waist. Crystal buttons adorn the right shoulder and top of the bodice, trickling down to peek out from ruffles on the left side of the gown.

Once again, proportion will be the key for this dress. While most petite women would shy away from an ample skirt, I'm giving the illusion of a massive dress without overwhelming the duchess' frame.

I have never made anything this, well, outstanding. I can't stop staring. I sort of want to put it on and never take it off. I can picture myself lounging around my apartment in it. Oh wait, I no longer have an apartment. Cancel that dream.

I take a minute to look around the workroom. We're finishing the final fittings. There's a lot of black in this room. Sancere's dress is all rainbow sequins, and they sort of remind me of fish scales, but I don't want to tell her that. Mine is the only pastel dress. There are a few in dark jewel tones. Either I'm a shoo in, or I totally missed the mark.

I chose pastel because I think the duchess is still rather young. She'll have her whole life to wear dark matronly colors. Plus, in the pre-wedding arena, I want to keep things light and festive. Beautiful Swarovski-crystal-studded shoes complete the outfit, with matching jewelry. I assume she might have real ice to wear, but I want to show how the dress looks all blinged out. Youthful, fashionable, yet old Hollywood.

My back is sore, and my fingers are literally bleeding. It's a wonder I have any sensation left in my fingertips after repeatedly poking them with pins and needles. Weyler actually cut herself, requiring a medic to come check her hand. We actually do put our blood, sweat, and tears into these projects.

You know, you'd think with only six of us left, the judging process would take less time. Somehow, it doesn't. At least it doesn't feel like any less time. I guess the initial presentation is shorter. This show appears more dramatic though, with swooshing skirts, sweeping trains, and shimmering sequins. Watching the gowns go up and down the runway, I can't help but feel that maybe Sancere is off target. Either she is or I am. Other than that, it's anyone's game.

Waiting to find out who's on the rack, we're quite subdued as compared to previous rounds. Maybe it's because there are fewer people. But I think it has more to do with the amount of work we've done in the past forty-eight hours. I'm spent, and looking around the room, I know I'm not the only one. Even Asher, who usually looks so composed, is showing fatigue around his eyes.

He's on the couch, opposite me. Lexington has planted himself firmly next to him and is glaring at me. Ash can't see that, of course, and is smiling in my general direction. This is a triangle that I don't think I want any part of. I can't help but give myself a mental pat on the back for the focus I've displayed over the past two days. It's amazing what I can accomplish when I don't let things—people—distract me. I wonder why it is that I've never had this sort of dedication in my life previously.

What would I do if I won *Made for Me*? First thing, hands down, is sleep for about a week. I've never felt fatigue like this before. Never. After that, and all the whooping and celebrating, I'd go home to see my family. Picking at my black knit skirt, my mind continues to wander. If I'm lucky, Mom will put together a big party, and there will be her cannoli cake, which is to die for. She only makes it on special occasions, but I think this would qualify. My body stills, realizing what I just did. This is the problem with me. Well, one of the many. I bury myself so deeply in the short-term details that I fail to see and plan for the big picture.

I need to look beyond the cake, no matter how good it is. And boy, is it good.

Winning the show means not only fifteen minutes of fame—I wonder if I could get on *Dancing with the Stars?*—but a contract to be Duchess Maryn's personal designer for a year. That includes all-expense paid trips to Montabago as needed. I'm really going to have to do some research to find out where in the world that actually is. And then there's the money. One-hundred thousand dollars. It's a big cash prize.

My debt would be gone. I could move out. Again. I could use some of the money to put into New Michele Designs so that I could be self-sufficient. After my year is up designing and creating the duchess' wardrobe, I could look at expanding my own business.

Holy crap, I think I've got a plan. It's like I'm an adult or something. Of course, it all hinges on me winning. I'm only half-way there. And as much as I love my gown, if the duchess and judges don't love it, all of this ends. And none of my problems will be solved.

Winning would certainly be the easy way out.

"Earth to Vanilla, come in Vanilla." Fink's grating voice interrupts my adulting. "We have to go back in for the rack."

I look at her blankly.

"Yeah, I'd be nervous if I were you too." She turns and disappears through the door into the presentation room. I hate her. I hate her with the passion of a thousand suns, and I'd throat punch her if it wouldn't get me kicked off the show. We had to sign a contract promising no physical confrontation. Stupid contract.

Passing through the door into the presentation room, I try to calm my nerves. I may have to find an outlet elsewhere. I can't help but glance in Asher's direction. Hmmm....

Looking around the room I do a quick head count. One ... two ... six. There are only six of us left. Will they still do three on the rack and then the three top designs? Will tonight be another double elimination? We're about to find out. The production assistants rearrange us in the seats so that we're three in the front and three in the back. The empty chairs sit, reminders of those who have gone before. The damask slides under my thighs, feeling rough and smooth at the same time due to the design. If I never see a light blue chair like this again, it will be too soon. I'd never thought myself prone to anxiety, but this show is doing a nice job of creating some—a lot—for me.

Callie Smalls enters without her usual fanfare. She makes her way over to us, the lowly contestants, and sits down. Is she actually going to make small talk? At first I think she is. Except there's only one of us she's talking to—Asher. A wave of something passes over me. Not jealousy per se, but something akin.

I try to shake it off, but let's face it, I'm not that big a person. Literally. Flopping back in my chair, I may have let out a small sigh. Sancere, seated to my right, leans into me.

"I know honey. He's a tough one."

"Is it that obvious?"

"Well, the two of you sucking face the other night was a little hard to miss. Quite entertaining, but hard to miss."

I bury my head in my hands. No, I will not let this get me down.

"Michele, are you okay?"

"I will be," I say, sitting up. I roll my shoulders back and try to make myself as tall as I can be. Asher's ahead of me to the left, and Callie's on the other side of him. Once again, his arms are draped casually across the backs of the chairs on either side of him, with his legs crossed and a relaxed posture. This appears to be his favorite sitting position. Like he doesn't have a care in the world. I bet he's never had a moment of discomfort in his life.

I wish I could stop staring at the backs of their heads, but I can't. No more than I can control the glare that I'm sure is on my face. Sancere pats my leg. "He's got that je ne sais qua, n'est pas?"

My high school French seems like eons ago, but even I remember how that expression is used to describe the indescribable thing that makes a person special. On the exhale I say, "He does. He's out of my league, and not my type. I know I'm not his, but I keep hoping."

A tiny furrow, betraying a strong dose of Botox, forms at the top of Sancere's nose. "Why do you say you're not his type? You look adorable together."

The seats are in much-too-close proximity to tell Sancere about my insecurities in regard to Asher's sexuality. I especially don't know how to broach that with Sancere in light her own status. Additionally, I think I noticed Asher's head cock slightly, ear in my direction.

I'm saved, as Callie elegantly stands up. The duchess and Taliance Ho file in, taking their seats opposite us. Callie's spiel for the camera is repetitive but soothing. My adrenaline courses as my gown swishes down the runway. However, seeing the others, my heart drops. I have no idea how this one is going to go.

Chapter 21

"Are you ready for your last assignment before the finals?" We're standing in the bedroom area of a furniture store. French-style furniture looms heavy, draped in silks and chiffons, which flutter slightly in the breeze created by some low-lying fans.

Lexington and Weyler are on my left, Fink and Asher on my right. Sancere was eliminated following the formal gown assignment. She missed the mark with her sequined gown. We still know very little about Duchess Maryn, and even less about her betrothed, Prince Stephan. I think they like keeping us in the dark—makes for better drama this way. But if I had to guess, from watching her facial expressions and the looks she's picked, the duchess appreciates my retro style. She likes Ash's clean lines, clearly with an edge toward menswear, and Lexington's classic style. I can't figure out why Fink is still here, other than to torment me. Weyler has skirted by, no pun intended. She usually finishes in the middle of the pack, neither on the rack, nor on the dress form. With the last assignment, we were only shown the top two and bottom two. Weyler, again, was neither one.

Oh, did I mention that I won again?

This time, post win, I behaved myself. Without Kira to make sure I made it to bed unaccompanied, I had a nice cup of hot tea and retired. Alone. Not that I wanted to. I'm trying not to be impulsive for once. We'll see how it works. Or doesn't.

The cameras in place, we're huddled in a clump now by a massive armoire with gold-leaf detail. Looks like something that would have belonged to Louis the somethingth. Certainly nothing a young woman starting her life would care for. Well, at least nothing I would want. It makes me wonder about Maryn. What's her story? Her background. Is this a marriage of love or arrangement? Do they even still do that? Has she dated anyone else? Is she a virgin?

And then it occurs to me why we're in a boudoir-type setting. We're going to have to design ...

"You may be wondering why we're here today. You're about to find out." Callie Smalls addresses us only briefly before turning to the cameras and beginning her monologue.

"Today we're here for the last assignment before the stunning finale of *Made for Me*. As important as the wedding day—maybe even more—is the wedding night. The assignment tonight is for our designers to create the perfect wedding trousseau for Duchess Maryn to wear on her wedding night!"

Lingerie. Ugh.

This is going to suck so hard. Silk charmeuse is miserable to work with. Slippery and sliding, denying the grip of pins and showing every mis-stitch. I don't work with this type of material for good reason.

Not to mention the design. How the heck are we supposed to figure out what this woman wants to look like on her wedding night? Does she want to be a sinner or a saint?

And then, there are the problem area issues. Every woman has them. What are Maryn's? If we're going to design her underclothes, I feel like we should at least be on a first-name basis.

I'm sure the panic is showing in my eyes. I know it spills forth, as I voice all these concerns when I'm interviewed following our trip to the fabric store.

At least I'm pleased with my fabric choices. I went with a golden ivory silk, rum pink silk, and lace for accents. I'm going to have to construct good support for the girls. While I see that Fink purchased boning to do a corset, I'm going to steer in another direction entirely. Nothing but soft romance from me.

Except I'm not feeling very romantic. Rather, I feel like I want to puke. We've sketched our designs, bought our fabric, and done our pre-production interviews. It's about four in the afternoon, and they haven't let us into the workroom yet. They've got us contained in a small area, like some sort of holding cell. I want to get to work. I keep reworking the design in my head, fine tuning and tweaking the plan.

Weyler nudges me out of my zone and whispers, "I'm making a dash to the bathroom. Do you want to come?"

I nod, standing up. A small walk, no matter how small, will feel good. I'm sure to be bent over my table all night, wrestling with the slippery material. I bend backwards to stretch my body in anticipation.

Finishing up before Weyler does, I call to her. "I'll be out in the hall when you're done."

I start pacing outside the door. Fourteen steps up the hall, fourteen steps back down. I wonder why they're taking so long letting us get to work. What's the hold up? Don't they know how this is eating away at my already fragile nerves?

"Well, aren't you a sight for sore eyes! This is a good sign that you're still in production."

I whirl around and see Lincoln leaning against the wall, nonchalantly. He looks like he belongs on the cover of GQ. Damn, I ask myself again, when did he grow up? I want to run and hug him, but remembering the last time I tackled him, I show restraint.

But he doesn't. In three large steps, he's reached me and grabs me up in his arms, crushing me to his chest. I exhale, and for a minute all my stress and worry dissipates. So much so that tears fill my eyes and threaten to spill down my cheeks.

"Michele, are you okay? Did I hurt you?" He releases me from his embrace and takes a step back, his hands still holding mine.

"No," I sniffle. "I'm just homesick. That's all."

"It's only been about two weeks. Surely you've been away from home longer than that?"

"Of course. It's the imposed communication ban that makes it seem so much longer. And has it only been two weeks? I have no sense of time. What's the date?"

"March 16th."

That startles me. "Oh! My birthday is tomorrow!"

A wide smile spreads across his face. "Why do you think I came down here to find you? I've got something for you." As Lincoln glances down, I notice the bag he dropped when he hugged me. Unassuming grocery bag, with an unassuming plastic take-out container. Upon further observation, I can't control my grin.

"Is that what—"

"Yup. Tony was home last weekend. It's been in the freezer for you. I did some recon to find out when you'd be in the building."

"But how?"

"I had my friend tell me if you were available."

"Your friend—Lauren?" I think an evil thought in her general direction.

"Yeah."

"What's the deal? Are you two dating or what?"

"Why? Does it matter to you?" He's suddenly defensive. I don't want to upset him. Lincoln's always been so nice to me. That being said, I don't know if I want him being nice to her.

"It doesn't. She just didn't seem to like that I know you. Maybe a little possessive."

"Hmm, interesting. I'll have to think about that." He rubs his chin in a pensive manner. Well, a mock pensive manner, since there's clearly laughter in his eyes.

"Well, um, thanks for this." I hold up the bag. "I can't believe I'm going to be thirty. And all alone."

The last part slips out. Before I can recover, Weyler finally exits the bathroom. She looks from Lincoln to me and back again. "Dang, girl. You work quickly. What's Asher going to think?"

Lincoln looks at me, confusion in his eyes. "Asher? Who's—"

Before he can finish, Lauren comes storming down the hall. "There you are! I should have known." She looks from Lincoln to me and back. And, shockingly, she's pissed again. At me, not Lincoln of course.

156

"This doesn't look good for you. People are already talking that you cheated your way onto the show because you're connected." I'm not sure if she's talking about herself or Fink, but I hope no one else really thinks that. She glares at me. Miraculously, her gaze softens as she looks at Lincoln. "Lincoln, I'll meet you downstairs at eight tonight. Are you in the mood for Chinese?"

Lincoln looks nervously at me. He hates rice. It's a long story involving him and Tony, of course, and a science experiment gone terribly wrong. A slow smile spreads across my face, knowing his secret. "Um, sure. I guess."

Lauren grabs my elbow, a little too firmly, if you ask me. "We're ready to head back to the apartments now."

Weyler has to run to catch up. "Aren't we getting to work tonight?"

"No, they announced that, but you two missed it." She sounds like an impatient school marm.

"So what happened then?" It's my turn to get impatient.

"The producers and judges were not in agreement on how much time you should get for this assignment. If you started tonight, you would either have too much or too little, depending. They decided to give you a night off and have you start tomorrow. The assignment will end at noon the following day, with judging right after that. The duchess will not be modeling these garments, for obvious reasons."

I blush, that thought filling my mind. As uncomfortable as I might be with this assignment, it's got to be even worse for Duchess Maryn.

As much as I was ready to get to work, I'm even more ready to go back to the apartment and savor my snack.

My mom's homemade cannoli cake. It's like she knew. Of course she did. The tears that had threatened in Lincoln's embrace spill out, uncontrollably now. Last year, for my birthday, Christine and I made the rounds of a few local bars. Since the day of my birth coincided with the feast day of St. Patrick, the bars were always packed. We ended up in some dive bar. But it was great, because she ran into Patrick, the guy she'd been mooning over since meeting him on the ski slopes the January before. I wonder how they're doing. They've been together officially for three months now.

I wonder when they're going to get engaged. It's not an if; it's a when. One glimpse of them together told me that. More tears fall, as I miss my best friend. I want to hear her voice and find out how things are in her blissful world. And when we can start planning her wedding.

I eat my cannoli cake, still cold from the freezer, and pull out a sketch book. I rough sketch out the gown I made for Christine last October, when she and Patrick were supposed to go to the Halloween party as Indiana Jones and Marion Ravenswood. For some reason or another, it didn't happen, but re-creating the gown from the movie was so much fun. Christine is the perfect canvas for a wedding gown. Really, for any clothing. I wonder if she'll let me make her wedding gown. Well, she doesn't really have a choice. I'm going to do it anyway.

I flip to a blank page and can barely control my pencil. The ideas flow and before I know it, Christine's wedding gown is staring back at me.

Now, if only I can convince her of that too. While I'm at it, I start to envision what I'm going to look like on that day. My guess is that I'll be in a soft mossy green, as it's Christine's favorite color. It's not the most flattering on me, but it is about her that day not me.

Before I know it, I've got the bridesmaids' dresses sketched. Four styles, all different but complementary. Christine works in the wedding planning business, so I know she'll have a good handle on flowers and table settings and venue. But this, I've got covered.

Dang, I miss my friend. I wonder if the producers would let me call her tonight, since it's my birthday in a few hours and all. It's worth a shot. I want to call my mom too, and thank her for the cake. I ate every single bite of the three-portion serving she sent.

I can't believe Lincoln did this for me. I can't believe he's going out with that horrid Lauren tonight. I can't believe how much it bothers me that he is. It shouldn't matter to me. Lincoln's just my friend. Not even my friend really, my cousin's friend. But I know that's not really true. Lincoln's my friend. Like my brother. Except when he was hugging me, it didn't feel like a brother. Not even close.

I'm in my tank and boxers, all ready for bed, hair piled on top of my head in a messy bun. Regardless, the urge to try and contact home is too strong. I head out to the living room to see if there's anyone left from the production crew. What I don't expect is a full-on party.

"SURPRISE!!!!!!"

The remaining cast and crew throw confetti and balloons in my general direction. Asher steps up and puts a party hat on my head, his fingers trailing down along my cheeks and under my chin as he adjusts the strap. I'm pulled into his gaze.

"But ... but ... how did you—"

"You said last week. I pulled a few strings. It's not every day a girl turns thirty." He leans in and gives me a soft kiss on the cheek. Not pulling away, he breathes softly, "Happy birthday, One-sixteen."

Lexington breaks the moment by saying boisterously from the couch, "Hell, but it is every year that I turn twenty-nine. Again."

Laughter erupts throughout the room. Who knew there were this many members of the production team? Apparently, the thought of free booze at the company's expense was enough to make them stay after hours.

Except for Lauren who is, of course, out with Lincoln. A stab through the heart again. I don't know why. Maybe because I wish Lincoln were here with me, a link to home.

Chapter 22

My back hits the bed with a solid thud, as Asher's weight presses down on top of me.

"Don't stop that!" I exclaim breathlessly.

"What this?" He does that thing with his tongue at the base of my ear. "Or this?" His hands are up under my tank, having freed my breasts from the confines of my bra.

"Yes, both. Oh my God." Now one hand is wandering down my thigh, and I don't want him to stop that either.

I didn't even drink that much, which is probably more than I can say for Asher, the rest of the cast, and most of the crew. Tomorrow's filming should be interesting. Tomorrow. I will have to face him in the morning.

"Ash—ASH—stop for a minute!"

He pulls his head off my neck and looks at me, his pupils narrow and lips full. "You told me not to stop."

"I know, but—didn't we agree not to do this while we're competing?" He shifts slightly, his manhood pressing into my thigh. Dang, that's even more of a turn on.

He leans back in for a little nibble on my ear. "I know, but I want to."

Sighing, I say, "So do I. But I don't want to."

He pulls back. "Oh, I didn't realize that." He sits up and turns away, indicating the hurt I've caused.

I sit up too, putting my arms around him. "No, that's not what I mean. Of course I *want* to. I'd be crazy not to. I think every person on the cast and crew wants you."

"But do you?" He still won't look at me.

"Asher, you have to understand—I make bad decisions. All the time. I'm impulsive and shortsighted and just do what feels good. And I know this would feel good. I need to make sure, for once in my life. Lord knows, I really want to though."

He turns so I can see his profile, and there's a hint of a smile. "I guess that makes sense."

"Will you stay in here with me?"

"Do you expect me to behave?" The devilish grin spreads across his face. There's a hint of arrogance. He's used to getting what he wants.

"A little."

"A little?"

"Well, it's not like I'm a nun, and Lord knows, I've got no willpower. But I'm gonna try."

His lips are on mine again. "Well, then, so am I."

****

I want you to know nothing happened. Well, not nothing. See aforementioned comment about me not being a nun. Some bases were reached, but Asher didn't get to home plate. I'm not that kind of girl. Truthfully, I am, and there's nothing wrong with that, except it messes with my head and heart, and I've neither the time nor the energy for that at the moment.

But this is good. This morning, I feel good. I can look myself in the mirror and be okay. Plus, we're making lingerie today, and that was all the inspiration I needed. Asher is sex in a can.

Whatever that means. That's one of Aunt Rosalie's sayings. I never quite got it before, but I think it fits here.

And I'm sort of okay with turning thirty. Sort of.

I've got my designs in focus and I'm ready to go. I'd love to do stockings and garters, but they might be too far beyond my capabilities. I bought the materials, should I have the time to tackle them. Definitely saving that for last.

I'm making three—well, technically four—pieces. A strapless bralette and panties, a short nightgown, and a long sweeping robe. Should the duchess be feeling frisky, she can just go with the undergarments and drape the robe for effect. All are vintage-style, reaching back to the 1940s when sexy wasn't about how much skin you could show.

I thought about doing a bustier or corset, but those are hard to get into and sometimes even harder to get out of, though the dukes and marquises in romance novels never seem to have any difficulty disrobing their virtuous ladies. I don't know what Prince Stephan's dexterity's like, but I've known many a man who was clumsy with a regular bra and completely flummoxed by a front closure one. Although I did have a guy friend who used to say he preferred the front hook bras, as he likened doffing one to "opening a book." That's neither here nor there, and

I'm not counting on the prince to have that much skill.

Although I hope for Maryn's sake, he does. A blush creeps over my cheeks, thinking about the skill level of someone else in this room. Crap. I need to focus. I cannot afford to be distracted like this.

Okay, so back to the task at hand. The bralette is strapless and extends about four inches down under the cups. It's a cropped version of a bustier, and infinitely more comfortable. While there is a little bit of boning for support, it's nothing that will prevent the duchess from important things, like bending and breathing. The underwire support will keep the girls nice and perky under the nightie. The panties are actually more of a brief. But these are not your mama's briefs. Well, they could be, but they're not granny panties. High waisted with a spandex panel right in front of the tummy, because who doesn't need that? They're very forties, so the bottom of her cheeks will peek out slightly in the back. Think what Marilyn Monroe would have worn. Her belly button won't show—just a few inches of skin around her midsection. Demure but very provocative all at the same time. For these I'm using ivory satin and spandex with the champagne pink lace. I'm so in love with them that I may have to make a set for myself.

The nightgown will skim the top of Maryn's knees, showing her lower legs, which have looked to be quite shapely. The top is satin, which gathers above the bra cup in a flirty chiffon bow. Above the bow, the satin fans out, sitting wide on the shoulder. Below the empire waist, the garment is the same ivory chiffon as the bows. In case you were wondering, silk chiffon is the devil's fabric. No wonder it's used in lingerie. The fun—and sin—experienced while wearing it does not make up for the hell one goes through to sew it.

I take my time, making the machine needle crawl along, stitch by stitch so as not to pucker or pull the delicate fabric. FYI, this is why these wispy scraps of fabric cost so much. No one in their right mind would use this material unless they were getting paid a handsome sum.

The robe, made of the champagne pink silk, is something right out of a Lauren Bacall movie. Slightly puffed sleeves that fit snugly just above the elbow. The structured shoulders giving definition and power. A deep, plunging neckline that meets below the breastbone where a trail of fabric covered buttons take over, trailing down the front.

There is no need for stockings and garters. My pieces in ivory and pale pink—these are perfection. At least in my eyes. They are demure but sultry. Clean but seductive. Pure but naughty. Retro but relevant.

They are the best things I've ever made, and I want to stare at them all day. As much as I despise working with the delicate, enigmatic fabric, it's all been worth it.

If I go home, I'm taking these with me. And I'm going to put them on and never take them off. That is, until the right guy wants to take them off.

Whoever that may be.

Chapter 23

My mom, and certainly my aunts, would never say that I'm conservative. Certainly not when it comes to sex. I'm pretty sure they all say novenas for me on a regular basis. Even compared to Christine, I'm not reserved.

They should meet some of the other contestants.

First and foremost, I feel bad for the models. There's not a whole lot of coverage with most of these creations, so they require some interesting tape jobs. And let me say, some areas should never have tape on them. I think the neighboring waxing salons got a fair bit of business in preparation for this show. All I can say is, some of the wedding night ensembles ... yikes.

It's not like I think the duchess has been saving herself for marriage. I'm still not sure how old she is, but she's older than sixteen for sure. So, it's a safe bet she doesn't need to wear pure white. That being said, I'm not sure she wants her trousseau to play double duty if she should ever get a job at Night Moves.

Maybe I am old fashioned. Not as old fashioned as the previous generation of females in my family, but in relation to my contemporaries. I think the wedding night should be romantic and pretty. Not involving whips and chains.

Okay, no one went that far, but I think maybe they could have. Fink definitely could have. Her corset is black leather. There are silver zippers and some chains. It is not at all what a bride would envision. Well, at least not a traditional bride.

Or maybe they do, and I've no idea how freaky some people like to get. Either way, all of the confidence I'd possessed has now flown out the window as crippling self-doubt seeps in and takes over.

Lexington's look involves a lot of red lace, and not much else. I didn't know the super-high French cut look was still in, but somehow Lex has made it work.

Weyler went full-on bustier, G-string, and stockings. Makes me glad I didn't attempt them. From the runway, it looks like she may have had some difficulties with execution, which was what worried me as well. The balcony bra top leaves little to the imagination, and frankly I'm afraid we're going to have a nip slip on television.

Asher's piece is ... seductive. He did a nightgown. Sort of. At least I'm not the only one who did more than skimpy under things. But his piece and mine, well, they're totally different. He went with a blue, about the blue of Maryn's eyes. Definite points on that one. From the front, the nightgown isn't too risqué. Not too much. There's a slight drape to the front neckline, hanging low enough to show some décolletage. Then, it's body conscious as it skims her mid-section and over her hips. It's a bias cut, which to me always feels sultry. And of course, the slit up the leg, pretty much to the groin. I'm pretty sure she's wearing a G-string. I hope she is. But when the model turns around, that's when you see where Ash has upped the ante.

The back drapes down in a dramatic cowl, all the way to her waist. Peeking through is a wide band of lace, like the back of a bralette. A silver heart adorns the top of the lace, right in the center of her back.

Damn, I wish I'd designed this. More like I wish I owned it.

As his model struts down the runway, Ash looks over at me and winks. My mouth goes dry as my face flushes. His eyebrows lift slightly, and if I'd previously missed his message, I'm reading it loud and clear right now. This outfit is for me.

Yowzas.

That's a lot of pressure.

Lucky for me, I don't have a lot of time to ruminate about Asher. With only five of us left and the duchess not wearing our outfits, the time between the runway and the presentation is much shorter. We eat, use the bathroom, and I barely have time to nap when the PAs start herding us back into the presentation room.

This time, there are three shrouded forms. The three winning looks. Does that mean only three of us will move onto the final round? That's what they do on that other show that we've been given strict instructions not to mention by name. My guess is that two are going home. Or are being dismissed. Or placed in purgatory, or wherever ejected contestants go to wait and wallow, because I know for certain wallowing is what I'll be doing if I get the boot at this point.

The cameraman gives a signal, and Callie Smalls addresses us from the middle of the stage.

"Tonight we've a very special presentation. The designers have been tasked with creating a wedding night trousseau fit for a princess! Due to the delicate nature of the garments, Duchess Maryn has chosen not to model tonight. Looks from three of our five remaining contestants have been chosen. These looks represent the designers who will continue in the competition to design Duchess Maryn's wedding gown as she marries Prince Stephan and becomes the Princess of the United Republic of Montabago!"

There's no rack. There's only those who will go on and those who will go home. My look is so different, so conservative compared to the others that I'm freaking out. I'm actually numb. I didn't come this far to fail now. Not like any of us did. Asher's the only one who's already a successful designer in his own right, so we're all counting on this to make us. And praying it doesn't break us.

Callie's still talking. "Up to this point, the designers have been creating their works blind. They've been given very little information about the royal couple, especially the bride-to-be. That will change for the three designers moving on to the final round. Each one will get to interview the duchess and meet with her wedding planner to see if he or she can best capture the essence and feel of the wedding, which is sure to be the biggest royal nuptials since William and Kate!"

Well, that's good news. For once. I've started playing with different designs, based on the items Duchess Maryn's chosen in previous rounds. I've been on the mark most of the time. I do feel she's more conservative than avant-garde, but maybe she'll be trying to make a statement. I guess I don't need to worry about that until I know if my look is currently on a dress form.

"Tonight's format differs in that we will present only the three remaining looks. The other two looks are implied to be on the rack, and those contestants will be considered eliminated. Additionally, there will be no rank given to the three surviving looks. They are to be presented in random order, and no favorite look will be identified. Each designer moving on from this point forth will be judged solely on the wedding presentation. Former performance will not be considered."

WHAT? That's bunk! How can they do that to us? I won two assignments, and that won't give me any advantage over Weyler, who's won none? This sucks big time. Unfortunately, my face betrays my sentiments, and I notice a camera zooming in on me as I'm scrunching my nose in distaste. Great. I can only imagine how I'm being portrayed in post-production. I hope my friends and family know me better.

"Without further ado, I present to you the looks, in no particular order, that will take their designers to the finals of *Made for Me!*" Callie Smalls glides over to the mannequin on the left. A flourish of black satin covering reveals the black leather underneath. Damn. Fink.

How the heck could she have made it? That look belongs in an S & M club, not on a royal princess. Knowing that this look has made it immediately crushes me. If Maryn likes this, there's absolutely no way that my soft and romantic pink and ivory pieces would appeal to her. So, Maryn has a freaky side. Who knew?

Callie speaks. "The execution and construction of this look, especially the leather and boning is flawless. There is real craftsmanship in this work that is unusual to find in this day and age. Congratulations Fink. You will receive the opportunity to design Duchess Maryn's wedding gown."

I sneak a peek at Fink who is beaming a smug smile. What I wouldn't do to wipe that off her face. So, I'm guessing that Lex and Asher will be the remaining two looks. Lexington's creation is as in-your-face sexy as Fink's. Asher's is so beautifully seductive that I don't know how she wouldn't choose it.

Callie floats to the next dress form. The cloud of black satin floats away to reveal the blue silk of Asher's design. Of course. "The next designer competing in the final is Asher. The judges were impressed with the sultry yet tasteful design, as well as the execution."

Now Callie's by the final shrouded form. I think I'm going to pass out. In my head I'm chanting, "It's not me. It's not me. It's not me." Obviously, I want this more than anything in the world, but I don't think I can deal with the crushing disappointment of not making it.

I squeeze my eyes shut. Every muscle in my body is clenched, trying to hold myself together. I think my heart is going to rupture through my chest, it's pounding so hard. I can't look. The rushing and pounding in my ears blocks out all sound. I think I'm going to pass—

And then I hear my name.

"The intricate simplicity, the vintage yet modern take on the bridal trousseau is why Michele has been chosen as the final designer to compete for the honor of designing Duchess Maryn's wedding gown!"

I'm in.

Chapter 24

The evening following the ceremony is bittersweet. Lexington is a blubbering mess, which makes me a blubbering mess as well. He may have resented the competition for Ash's affections, but I really like him. I don't want him to go. Weyler's bit her lower lip nearly in half trying to control the quivering and shaking. I didn't have tons to do with her, but I understand how devastating this has to be.

It's devastating for me that Fink is left.

She's glaring at me. I absolutely do not know what I could have possibly done to make her hate me so. Yes, I'm vanilla and conservative. It's not a condemnation of her slutty—I mean adventurous-style. I know she wants to believe that my connection to Lincoln got me a place on the show, but she knows as well as I do that it's not true. I've never spoken out against her, yet she's been on my case since day one.

Whatevs. She sucks.

Ash is looking at me expectantly again. What's life going to be like when I'm not seeing him every day? Will we stay in touch? Will he forget all about me? Can I handle that?

I know I could. But is that what I want? I'm thirty now. Crapola. I'm like actually thirty. It's time to start getting my act together.

We're crashed on the couch, my legs draped lazily over Ash's lap. Fink's in her room. Fine by me. "What do you think the timeline for this will be? They can't just give us a few days, right?" That's been bothering me. I thought Callie Smalls had said something about a week, but even that's cutting it close to do such an elaborate project.

Ash laughs. "Three weeks. Weren't you paying attention?"

"Have you met me? That's one of my largest challenges. I try, but my mind gets wandering. And even if I do hear something, I get nervous that I didn't hear it right, or I *think* I heard it one way, when it's really another. Like I thought she said three weeks, but then I started panicking that it was a figment of my imagination."

"Maybe you should write things down." Asher's rubbing my legs a little. Ahhh.

"I do, sometimes. And then I get paranoid that I wrote them down wrong."

"You need a personal assistant."

"I need someone to follow me around all the time and help me manage all the things I can't."

"Yeah, that's called a personal assistant."

I laugh. "Do you have one?"

"Trig and I used to share one. Daniel. I think Daniel solely works for Trig now. Mostly because I'm pretty sure I'm totally out." His demeanor changes, and I can tell this is hard for him.

"Are you okay? Do you want to be out?"

His shrug is meant to be careless, but I don't think it is. "I guess. You know how it is. The devil you know or the devil you don't. I think this is going to be good. I mean, I know it is. But ..." He trails off before he can finish. The only time I see any sort of doubt, any kind of vulnerability in Ash is when he's talking about his business. With people, he's so sure. Confidence oozes out of him. But this new venture, starting over, makes him nervous. "I don't like being alone."

And for some reason, that vulnerability in a world of bravado is all sorts of appealing.

"You're a fantastic designer. I'm sure whatever venture you decide to take on will be successful. People respond to you. You have this, this ..." I'm waving my hands about, trying to come up with a gesture that describes Asher. "This charisma. You charm everyone you talk to, even when you're not trying."

He leans back slightly into the corner of the couch so he's looking at me more. It's almost like I can see his shield coming back up. "Did I charm you?"

I feel my face growing hot. "Of course you did. Against my better judgment, you did."

"Why is it against your better judgment?" There's a playful smile on his face, but I can see the seriousness underneath. It flashes for a moment, and then he's hidden it again. The bravado is back.

I take a deep breath, not knowing where even to start. "We're on two totally different playing levels. You've already made it in the design world. I've sold five skirts on Etsy. You're from England, have moved to California, and are now planning world domination. I'm from Albany and couldn't hack more than a semester away from my family in Ohio. My family is sort of my everything, and I don't know that you've even mentioned yours. Oh, and then there's the sex thing."

He laughs in amusement. "That's quite the list. We can get back to most of these, but let's start with the sex thing."

I need a drink, or many, to have this conversation. I get up, pour myself a glass of pinot grigio and promptly down it. I refill my glass and resume my position on the couch, draped across Ash's lap.

He raises his eyebrows, encouraging me to start. Another deep breath. "I'm obviously not a virgin. I mean, I'm thirty years old." I trip a little getting that thirty out. It's still tough to process. "I've had relationships. I've had casual things. But I spent the past year being a booty call, thinking it would turn into more. Even though I tried to tell myself I wasn't, I was holding out unreasonable hope. So when I found out Barrett the rat got engaged, it sort of sent me into a tailspin. I'm so angry. At him, but more at myself. I was an idiot and I got played."

"Okay, but what does that have to do with me?"

"Well, you're so much more ... worldly ..." I can't think of how else to put it. "You have a lot of *experience* that I don't, and never will."

"You're not bi."

"And you are."

"Does that bother you?"

My silence is all the answer he needs. The disappointment is written all over his face. "I don't want it to, but it does. It's the trust thing. Like, if you're out with your guy friends, how do I know you won't ... you know?"

"It's called trust."

"Right. And I'm being upfront with you that it's something I have issues with. Barrett got engaged, came over and visited me the next day, and then within a week was planning his wedding. I had no idea that he was even seeing someone. I thought the reason we broke up the last time is that I was pushing him into doing something he didn't want to do."

"What was that?"

"Meet my family."

Asher laughs. "That's nothing. A little tea and cake with Mum and Dad. Who can't get through that?"

It's my turn to laugh. "No, you don't understand my family. We're big and loud and we're all up in each other's business. There's very little separation between where one family starts and another ends. My aunts are like my other mom, and my cousins are like my siblings. In fact, I'm closer with some of my cousins than I am with my own brothers. And friends of the family aren't friends—they're family. It's messy, and complicated, and they make me want to scream, but I wouldn't want anything different."

"Yeah, that's a bit different. I can see why someone wouldn't want a lot to do with that."

"But if the options are dealing with that or not having me, I guess I would want that to be a more difficult choice than it seemed to be for Barrett the rat."

"I think you're worth a few evenings of discomfort a few times a year."

"Gee thanks. At least there's good food. And football, usually."

"American football?"

"Of course. Although my dad and uncles and brothers and cousins do watch quite a bit of soccer too."

"Football."

"No, soccer."

He smiles. "See, there may be more important difficulties than the whole bi thing. And I'm going to say this about that and then it's done. I don't limit myself. I'm attracted to people, to their souls and their personalities. The gender thing is just an aside. So if I'm attracted to you, then it's only *you* I want to be with. That's all."

"But what about Lexington?"

"What about him?"

"You were very flirty with him."

"He's a terrible flirt, and that's fun. He's attractive, don't you think?"

"Of course. Anyone with eyes can see that."

"I'm not getting my knickers in a knot that you find someone else attractive, am I?"

"It's different. He's not interested in me; I'm not interested in him. Lex was definitely interested in you."

"He's certainly pretty and funny, but he's not who I'm attracted to at the moment. He's not you."

Well, that settles that. Discussion done.

Chapter 25

"You're not going to believe this. I'm coming home in three days!" I can't help but squeal as I finally hear Christine's voice. It's even better to see her face, grainy and pixelated as it is through the computer screen. Still better than nothing. It's been so long since I've talked to her. Well, in reality, it's only been a month, but time is super warped here. I feel like I've been away for four months.

"Is this a good thing?" Christine, as always, is cautious. I'm the one who moves with reckless abandon.

"Oh, yes, it's a good thing. Doing this show has been the best thing I've ever done."

There's an audible sigh. "I'm glad. I've been so worried that it wasn't going to go well. And you look tired."

"I can neither confirm nor deny whether it's going well, but I'll be home for a few weeks, and then back to New York for a bit." I glance over to the PA who's policing my call.

"I've been worried. I've heard these things can be stressful."

"Oh gosh, yes. While it's the best thing I've ever done, it's also the worst. The pressure is like nothing I've ever felt before. Well, that's mostly because usually

I don't actually push myself, but even for those who are driven, this is tough. And the ceremonies—I wanted to puke each time."

"I can see that. All those dramatic pauses."

"Exactly!!!! It's even worse in person. Like it takes sooooo long to film all that stuff. You don't know whether to go crazy with boredom or out of your mind with worry. Either way, it's not a comfortable place. But enough about me, what's going on with you? How's Patrick?"

"Are you okay?"

"Yeah, why? I just told you how I am. I want to know what's up in your life. I feel like I've missed out on so many things."

Christine is silent for a minute. I see her chewing the inside of her cheek. That's her tell for being deep in thought. Skype is good, but I wish we were together, having a cup of coffee. Or better yet, a big martini. Heck, even when we're in the same area, our schedules never quite mesh. I end up seeing her about five times a year. We had to plan a vacation together last year just so we could see each other. If I had money, I'd suggest we plan another trip. Of course, now she has Patrick, so our days of girls' trips are probably done.

"Um, I've got something to tell you." There's a serious tone to her voice. Not that there isn't always, but this is even more so.

"Oh my God, are you pregnant?" My voice rises about four octaves. It's sort of high to begin with, so I think only dogs may be able to hear me at this point. I start bouncing up and down in my seat.

"Calm down. God, no! Bite your tongue!"

"Then what?"

"Don't get mad at me. I know it's quick, and you like to be the impulsive one, but ..."

"You're getting married?" We've been friends for so long that it's not unusual for us to finish each other's sentences. Mostly because I'm too impatient to wait for Christine to finish.

"YES!!!!" This time, she's squealing in the dog-only octave. She starts waving her hand at the screen, but I can't see the ring. Mostly because there's too much movement.

"OH MY GOD!!!!" I'm jumping up and down and squealing too. It wouldn't surprise me if the glass around me shatters. "I knew it!"

"What do you mean, you knew it? How could you know it? I didn't even know it!"

I'm still jumping up and down. "I had this feeling a few days ago. Wait, when did it happen? Maybe I'm like psychic or something!"

"It just happened this morning. I ... I can't think straight right now. I'm practically speechless!"

"Wait, it happened today? But you let me do all the talking for most of this phone call." I look at the timer. There are only ten minutes left. "I've only got a few minutes."

"Okay, so then—"

"Yes and yes." I don't even let her finish. I know what she's going to say.

"How do you even—"

I cut her off again. "Yes, I'll be your maid of honor, and it's already done."

"What's already done?"

"Your wedding gown. I've already designed it.

Plus, I came up with what I would like my dress to be, but obviously you can tell me what you think."

"How ... when ... I don't—"

"I mean, we don't have to go with it, if it's not what you want, but ..."

"Do you have it there? Can you show it to me?" She's bouncing around again. She's not a bouncy person. This is without a doubt the most excited I've ever seen her.

"I don't have my sketch book, but I've got a piece of paper. I'll start drawing and you tell me what you want." I barely look at the screen as my hand flies over the paper. Still, I feel the need to talk as I draw.

"Tell me what you were thinking. Ball gown? Strapless? Halter? Train? Satin? Or something totally different, like a sexy sheath? Backless? Your back is gorgeous and you'll want to show that off. Oh, I do have to say, no gloves. That's like so 1990s. I cannot let you do that. Have you thought about color? Like a champagne or a blush? It would be different, but you know, white is so boring. And veil or no veil, because that makes a difference. Are you going to do a blusher? Chapel length? Cathedral length? What color were you thinking for the bridesmaids' dresses, because you know I look good in pink. It'll coordinate with the mossy green that you love, you know, to create contrast. And I ..."

"Stop! Just take a breath. There were too many words and I barely caught any of them. Now, go more slowly. Please. I've had a glass of wine. I can't follow that many words at once." I see her raise a glass of champagne and take another sip. "Now, what was all that?"

"Well, I know I'm tossing some ideas around, but you know, *technically*, it is your day and all. If you close your eyes and picture you walking down the aisle, what do you see?"

Christine takes a deep breath and closes her eyes. "You know, I'm sort of thinking lace. I don't think you said that in your barrage. And probably not strapless, but I don't want long sleeves either. Is there something in between that you can do? Like a sleeveless-type thing? I do like something fitted though. And I know this is crazy, but I don't know that I want a train. I know I'm supposed to, but it would be a lot of fabric to deal with, you know? But, like could you do a super long veil so I still have something trailing behind me when I walk down the aisle?"

I hold up the sketch, a virtual duplicate of what I'd drawn the first time. It's exactly what she just told me. Her mouth falls open. "Oh my God, you nailed it. I can't wait for you to get started!"

The timer goes off, and I have to end our session. All I want to do is make my best friend's dress. But I can't.

I've got another wedding gown to make first.

****

"Tell me about yourself."

I hate these open-ended questions. I never know how to start. Or when to stop. Or what to say in between. In all the interviews I've done for this show, my ability to make a fool out of myself has not diminished. In fact, I think it's risen exponentially. Add the fact that I'm in a private meeting, save the cameras, with a member of the royal family, and it spells disaster.

"I, um, ah ..." That's all I can manage. I trip over my tongue, like the idiot I am. I clear my throat and start again. "I'm horrible at interviews. I'm still not sure how I made this show. I don't think the panel was drunk or high, but they must have been. I don't know why else they would have chosen me."

Duchess Maryn laughs slightly. She's wearing a bit less makeup than during the show. I would estimate her age to be in the low to mid-thirties. She's wearing well-fitting khaki slacks and a polka-dotted top that buttons up. The collar ties, and she wears it loose, but not too low. She doesn't show off any cleavage. Good to remember. This is my chance to get to know her a little better, but once again, I'm barely coherent.

There's no way she's going to want to work with me to design not only her wedding gown, but to be her personal designer for the next year. I wouldn't want me.

"I'm sorry. I'm not very good with these things. You know," I nod over my shoulder, "the cameras freak me out. Even after all this time, I can't do it. I can't relax and be myself."

The duchess leans toward me and motions for me to meet her. In a whisper so low I can barely hear, she says, "Me too. I absolutely hate them. Hate, hate, hate. Steph thought this show would be a good way for me to get used to them." She glances around nervously. "I don't think it's working."

"But you always look so composed."

"Have you noticed I don't really speak? There's a reason for that."

"What are you going to do once you're married? Won't you have to do public appearances and everything?"

"Take lots of Valium?"

I laugh and ease back into my seat. I guess it's nice to know that I'm not the only bumbling idiot here. At least my lifetime won't be spent in the spotlight. Maybe, like if I'm successful enough, I'll hire people to handle all the business stuff and then I won't have to do more than sew.

"I thought it was just me. Everyone else seems so confident. I can speak to people one to one, but the cameras ... apparently they sap my brain cells."

"Well then, other than our mutual hatred of those soul stealers, what else would you like to tell me? How did you get into this business?"

I know I should put on a polished and professional veneer, but that doesn't work for me. I think, maybe Maryn and I could get along well. I decide to pretend we're already friends. "I'm not really in the business. I sew. I love to sew. It's all I want to do, other than hang out with my friends and family." I retell the story of my wayward attempt at design school, my dead-end position at U'nique Boutique that was ended by the wayward eye of its owner and my skanky co-worker. I even tell her about my significant lapses in judgment in relation to men (aka, Barrett the rat, among others) and my inability to efficiently plan my finances. "And that now has me living, at least temporarily, at Casa Mom and Dad, but even that's not going to work out. My mom's been so despondent about my lack of direction that she's started calling in to radio talk shows looking for career advice. Most of them tell her that I should go back to my college guidance office, but I can't even do that!" Jeez, I'm a loser.

"Wow, that's quite a story. You do have quite the passion for your work."

"I'd like to think I do. It's what makes me happy."

"Okay, well we should get down to business and talk wedding."

I shift forward a bit in my chair. I'm still clutching my sketchbook on my lap. Flipping it open and smoothing the paper, I'm ready. "I hope you don't mind if I write things down. It'll help me figure out what direction to take when designing."

"Your designs have been spot on so far. I love the classic, almost vintage style. Like I'm channeling Grace Kelly."

"I wish I could say that was intentional. In all honesty, that's my design aesthetic. It's where I like to be. Even when I try to be contemporary and modern, it comes out fifties."

"You need to be true to who you are."

"I guess. But this is about who you are. What are your visions for this wedding? I'm getting the classic vibe, obviously. Anything you want or want to stay away from?"

"It's so hard. Because, if I were marrying someone different, this isn't what I'd do at all. I'd go to a beach somewhere, just us. Obviously, that's not an option. I understand that there are duties and responsibilities, and I'm willing to take that on. He's worth it."

A small smile creeps across her face, like she's having a private moment, thinking about her fiancé.

"So this is a love match then?" I'd had doubts before, and now they're all erased.

She chuckles. "Most definitely. I wouldn't be going through all this if it wasn't. There's no money that's worth the invasion of privacy. I don't understand people who strive for fame. It's terrible."

"I used to think it would be fun. Now I'm not so sure. I mean, the lifestyle here—I could get used to it. Everything's so nice! And there's this rain head shower that's totally amazing, and since I'm not paying for water, I don't feel guilty staying in there for a while. Of course, when we have five a.m. calls, and there were all of us who needed to shower, I didn't get to spend as long as I would have wanted."

Maryn looks at her watch. I think it's diamond encrusted. It's hard to tell since I'm blinded by the rock on her hand. Four carats, easy. "We don't have tons of time, so let's get down to business. May I take a look at your book? I'd like to see how your process works."

I hand it over to her without thinking, and then sit back for a minute while she peruses through. I'm studying her bone structure and coloring, trying to commit it to memory. She's biting her lip slightly as she turns the pages, thoughtfully looking at my scratchings and drawings. Some aren't complete, just fledgling ideas for me to someday return to finish.

I'm thinking an off-the-shoulder look for the duchess. Just a hint of shoulder showing at the top.

She really does have fantastic collar bones. They're defined but don't give her an emaciated look. Delicate, feminine. I need to ask about her feelings on lace, because I'd ...

"Oh! You've already designed it! I love it! I ... I ... well, I find myself speechless!"

I'm not sure what she's talking about. She turns the book to me and my heart sinks.

That design is not for the duchess and certainly not for a TV show. That creation is for my best friend.

And now the princess-to-be wants Christine's dress.

Chapter 26

My stomach feels sick. Like, not hungover sick or bad Thai sick, but that deep pit that won't go away.

Christine already loves this dress, as do I. And I will never be able to picture my bestie in anything else. Not to mention the fact that Christine's about Amazonian height, and Maryn's a midget. Obviously not, since we're the same height, but the same proportions won't work for both. How do I tell the duchess that the style is all wrong for her?

I put Christine in a figure hugging mermaid-style dress. Bateau neckline. Sleeveless, as years of ballet justify her showing off not only her figure but her sinewy arms as well. White lace over a pale ivory satin, which is low cut in the back. The lace and sheer fabric overlays provide modesty while revealing sex appeal at the same time. Of course, buttons from the neck on down. No train as requested, because the flare of the mermaid skirt will suffice. A royal wedding historically necessitates a train. Maryn *needs* a train.

She closes the sketchbook and hands it back to me. "I love it already. I never would have thought that silhouette or sleeveless, but I feel like you know me so well. You certainly know what works on my body. I totally trust you, so if you feel that works, then run with it. After the lingerie assignment, I saw how you understand what my challenges are. Oh, that reminds me—if you can build support into the dress so I don't have to wear all those contraptions underneath, I'd appreciate it, if you know what I mean."

She winks at me, yet I still can't open my mouth for fear of vomiting all over her Louboutins. "Do you have any other questions for me? No? Well, it was smashing getting to talk to you. I have a feeling," she stares pointedly at the sketchbook that I'm crushing with my white knuckle grip, "that we'll be seeing each other in the future."

What am I going to do?

I know what I should do.

I also know that if I show up with a dress that looks anything different from the sketch, the duchess is likely to go full on bridezilla on me. At the very least, I'll lose the competition. Which would be okay, I guess, if I still have my integrity. But it's not like integrity is going to put a roof over my head or food in my mouth.

Well now crap.

I need to get some sleep, but it's eluding me at the moment. We're filming again in the morning, when the final round officially launches. I sort of wish they'd send us home for that last three weeks, like that other show does, just so I can be near my family. Maybe, if I were home, I'd be able use my mom's home cooking to bury my guilt at giving away my best friend's gown. Great—so I can be fat and a lousy friend. It's the perfect combination.

"Why so glum?" Asher flops on the bed next to me. It's never been agreed upon that we would be sharing a room—and bed—but that's what has somehow happened. Truth be told, I'm happy for the company. I'm still behaving myself, for the most part. "Didn't your interview go well? I think she's absolutely darling."

"I think your accent is absolutely darling. And the interview was fine. She's very nice. Relatable." I'm undecided as to whether I should tell Asher about the dress issue. Probably not. Some warning bell deep within the recesses of my brain is going off. He is my competition. I don't need him getting a look at my design. Especially if it's the one I'm going to go with.

"All you American chicks dig the accent. I could be the most homely chap ever, but the accent would win them every time."

I can't help but chuckle. Mostly because he's right. "What other general stereotypes do you have about American women?"

He brushes a stray hair from my eyes. "Mostly what I learned from that The Guess Who song. Like that I should probably be asking you to stay away, and all that."

The memory of that song floods me with nostalgia, making me laugh and tear up all at the same time. Since Asher's not in on the private joke, I feel the need to tell him. "My sister never quite knew what they were singing. For the longest time, she thought they were saying, 'Making a Waffle' instead of 'American Woman.' I don't know how she got that out of it, but we thought she was crazy when she'd talk about the waffle song. Then we realized the mistake she made. To this day, I can't hear the song without singing, 'Making a Waffle.'"

I miss my sister. I hope she's pregnant by now. I hope her kids do not get her song lyric interpretation skills. I miss my family. I miss home.

"Why are you so sad? Wasn't that supposed to be a funny story?" Asher wipes away the tear that's escaped the corner of my eye.

"I'm missing home again. I really hope we get to go home for the three weeks to work on the wedding gowns. I mean, how else are they going to keep us from seeing each other's work?"

"I guess. I'd be fine staying here."

"You would? Why?"

He shrugs, staring at some far off spot on the wall. "It's not like I have a great home to go to. Trig and I aren't really speaking, so it's not like anything appealing awaits me in California. And I don't consider England home anymore."

"I thought you're moving back; when this is all done?"

"Yes, but to London. I'm from Keswick."

My blank stare betrays my ignorance.

"It's in the Lake District."

Again, I've got nothing.

He sighs. "Bloody Americans. It's in the northwest corner, while London is in the southeast. They're almost five hundred kilometers apart."

Stupid metric system. I am a dumb American. "How far is that in American?"

"About three hundred miles. A good six-hour drive, if the weather's good. And usually it's not, considering the Lake District is the rainiest part of England. But still, it's great for all those outdoorsy types, which obviously I'm not. No, I will not be heading back there."

"Did you and Trig live together?"

"No, but we share a studio where I'd have to work. I suppose he could suck it up for the publicity. I'll make sure to get the company name in several times to shut him up."

"Were you, like partner-partners? Or just partners?"

"Is that like when you like someone, but you don't like them-like them, you just like them?"

"Sort of, and how do you know about that? It's a girl thing. And I would have thought an American thing. Maybe it's world-wide."

"No, it's an American thing. I came to the U.S. when I was about thirteen for boarding school. My dad had a job where he traveled quite a bit, and most of his work was based out of Connecticut. I was in a boarding school from thirteen until I graduated high school. Even though I was pretty close, I still never saw my parents much. I think it made them feel better to say I was nearby."

"Oh, that's awful!"

"Not really. It was pretty great, actually. And back to your earlier question, Trig and I were never partner-partners. He's not my type."

"Why? I thought everyone was your type."

"And there you go stereotyping again. I said I'm attracted to the personality. The soul. Trig's personality leaves a lot to be desired. He makes me look humble and unsure."

"Then why did you go into business with him?" I've settled myself in the crook of Asher's shoulder, and I'm pretty darn comfortable. I could cuddle like this forever.

"Because he's a feckin' fantastic designer. I knew he was going to be successful as long as he could keep his ego in check. Turns out, my primary job has been reigning in that ego. And I'm done. If he crashes and burns now, it's all his doing. He should listen to me about where to take the business. I not only have a degree in fashion design, but an MBA from Columbia. I sort of know what I'm talking about. But will he listen? Nooooo. It's his way or the highway. So I hit the road."

"Oh, that's terrible. I don't think I could work like that."

"I tried, because he is so insanely talented, but I just couldn't do it anymore. I do think I could spin my departure so the company would get a fair amount of publicity. He'd probably go for that. He's not business savvy, but he understands press."

"I hope it works out. That you find a place to work."

"What about you? Where will you be?"

"I'm at my parents' house. Maybe they'll let me set up in the basement. There's a pool table down there, but we hardly ever use it anymore. I bet I could move things around. Or they might have even sold it. They're downsizing this summer, so I think a lot of stuff's got to go anyway."

He starts to sit up, forcing me to abandon my position on his chest. "I've got a brilliant idea."

Now we're awkwardly sitting on my bed, and I'm pretty sure my hair is standing straight out where I'd been laying on him. He pauses for a minute and then starts. His eyes are glittering, replacing the normal reserved look with excitement. "I think you should come to London with me. Your business is internet based, no? You can work from anywhere. I'm starting over, you're starting over. We can start over together."

Have I mentioned that I tend toward the impulsive side? Before I can put on a cool, calm composure, I find myself literally jumping up and down on the bed. "Oh my God, do you mean it? You can't be serious! Please be serious!"

Never does it occur to me that London is really far away. I'm too overwhelmed with the excitement of the proposal, like the hottest guy in school just asked me to the prom.

Perhaps in an effort to spare me from making a complete and total fool out of myself, Asher pulls me back down onto the bed, wrapping me in his arms and kissing me senseless. Not that I had much sense to begin with.

"Is that a yes?"

"Of course it's a yes! I've never been to London."

"You'll need to get a passport as soon as you can. That can take a while sometimes."

"Oh, that I actually have. Christine and I went to Cabo last year. It was a great trip. And now, she's getting married! I'm going to have so much to do for that."

"Will you be designing her dress as well?"

"Yeah and I—" I stop myself from telling him the predicament I'm in. I'd forgotten about it for a few moments. "I'll have to work on that once my mind is clear."

Ash kisses me again. "From what I've seen, your mind is never clear. It's always whirling here and there and in about a million different directions all at the same time."

"Is it that obvious?"

"Only because I've had my eye on you. When you work, though, you have absolute focus. It's almost scary."

"Scary? That's how a girl wants to be described."

"You know what I mean. You're totally in the zone. It's impressive. I'm frankly a little jealous."

"You, jealous of me? You're crazy." We've settled back down, and I give him a playful slap.

"I know. That's why I asked you to come to London with me."

Chapter 27

"Our final three contestants are gathering for the last time before they see each other at the final competition."

Thank you Callie Smalls, for clearing that up. Looks like I'll be heading home to work on Maryn's wedding gown. Part of me is relieved. Super relieved. I still don't know what I'm going to do about Christine's dress. Being in a familiar, comfortable setting will let me make the best decision. I hope.

"We will gather for the final judging in three weeks, at which time the designs will be presented. The winner, however, will not be announced at that time. Tune in the following evening for coverage of the royal wedding between His Royal Highness Prince Stephan and Duchess Maryn Medrovovich."

Callie smiles her plastic smile for the camera until she's given the cut sign. Her face falls back into its resting, expressionless position and she turns to us. "We'll of course tell you the winner. He or she will be flown to Montabago to attend the wedding as an honored guest. Obviously, he or she will also be responsible on the day of the wedding for any last-minute needs the duchess may have."

Holy crap, this is getting real. I know there's a time lag between the taping of the show and its airing, but we still only have a few weeks to put a wedding look together. Soup to nuts, foundation garments to veil. Oy vey. I may need to start hyperventilating.

The only thing that prevents me from needing a paper bag is an unintentional glance at Fink. She's sitting there with a smug look on her face. This isn't phasing her in the least. I don't know how she does it. How she never lets anything get to her.

The camera people adjust some things, and the light crew shifts position. Callie readjusts, makes sure no wrinkles have reappeared, and squares her posture. She nods to the head camera guy and begins. "These three designers, Asher, Fink, and Michele—" the camera focuses on each of us as she says our names. I try to sit up tall, wipe the worried look from my face, and suck in my stomach. Damn craft services. "—have been focusing on designing a wedding gown for Duchess Maryn. They've met privately with the duchess to discuss her likes and dislikes."

Yeah, her like is the gown I designed for my best friend that is the total wrong style for her. Her dislike is any other gown I may design.

"However, there's more to the assignment than that. The designers will also have to create the wedding day looks for the attendants, both sides."

What the— ? I think I'm going to be sick. Not only do I have a mere three weeks to create the perfect wedding dress for a princess, but now I have to design and make bridesmaids' and groomsmen's outfits too? I need a puke bucket. Pronto.

The cameras zoom in, reminding me that they want to see the shock on our faces. They'd probably love it if I hurled on camera. Well, not *on* the camera, but you know what I mean.

Then it occurs to me—what if it's a massive wedding party? How am I supposed to make twelve dresses and suits, in addition to the wedding gown? And a suit? I know nothing about men's suits.

Heck. They just handed this contest to Asher. I glance over at him, and, as usual, his expression exudes confidence. Why am I the only one freaking out here?

"To handle the volume of this task, an assistant will be provided for each contestant."

I feel some relief wash over me. Callie disconnects her mic for a moment as the crew rushes busily to the other side of the presentation room. The lighting is shifting around again, and it looks like they're getting ready for a runway presentation. After a few minutes, Callie gets the nod again and plugs back in. "Each contestant will choose one assistant ..." she waves at the curtain, which is swishing and swaying. Suddenly, the curtains part, and all the eliminated contestants walk out onto the runway. I can't help myself from squealing and clapping a bit.

Oh, but now this requires strategy. I need to pick someone who not only has strong skills but who I can work with as well. There's really only one choice for me—Kira. I look around to see what Fink and Asher are doing. And that's when I see it. Fink's watching me. That ho is going to steal whomever I want to choose. It's written on her face, plain as day. How do I stop her from sabotaging me?

I look over at Ash, who simply smiles in my direction. I know he's going to pick Lexington. I lean over Fink and whisper loudly, "Who are you going to choose?" I hope this plan works.

"Probably Lex, unless you want him." He winks at me.

"I'm going to pick Weyler. She almost made it into the finals, and her sewing ability is very strong. That's what I need, someone who can help me with that." Weyler is boring and uninspired and will offer nothing in the way of creative input, but I don't mention that.

"Sounds like a good plan."

"I think so. It will be perfect."

Fink is sitting there, still as a corpse while this exchange goes on. I see the hint of a smile form at the corner of her lips, and I think I've got her. I hope this works.

The camera zooms in on us, and then it pans the runway. Callie's standing in the middle of the motley crew of ousted designers. "Now, the remaining contestants will pick one of the eliminated contestants to be their assistant for the final assignment. Asher, we'll start with you."

Asher stands and smiles. "Lex, old boy—wanna give it a go?" Lexington jumps up and down and claps a bit.

"Fink, who is your choice for assistant?"

She stands, and I can see her glance down on me. "I choose ... Weyler."

Weyler looks a bit shocked. She tries to cover by nodding and smiling slightly. I don't think she's thrilled. Oh well. Sorry to sacrifice her like this, but I'm in it to win it.

"And Michele, who will you choose to assist you?"

I stand up, confident for the first time in a while. "Kira! Roomies again?"

She gives me a big smile. "You know it!"

Game on.

Chapter 28

The show offers to put our assistants up in hotel rooms, but of course my mom won't hear anything of it. She's cleaned out my brothers' old room, and that serves as Kira's room. We spent the first day cleaning out the basement and moving my sewing things down there. The pool table, covered with a muslin-wrapped board, makes a good work surface on which to lay out my fabric.

The good news is there are only four attendants on each side, plus a ring bearer and flower girl. It could be a lot worse. The bad news is I still don't know how to make a man's suit, or how to make it stand out from all the other men's suits out there. Menswear is boring. Now I know why Asher wants to get out.

I love being home. I feel in my element. Maybe it's the food. My mom hasn't stopped cooking since I called her to tell her that I'd be returning. I've got my mission; she's got hers.

However, working at home is going to bring a new set of challenges. Namely, distractions. Anticipating how much of a time suck it could be, I had my mom take my computer away before I got home. I gave her my cell as well. I could see myself spending days combing the interwebs, looking to see what people have said about the show. And me. And

Asher. Before the show, I'd never have had the discipline to do that, but weeks without being connected have made it seem less important. Plus, there will be plenty of time to stew on that stuff once my work is finished. There are only so many days to get so much done. I'm sort of proud of my new-found focus.

The first day is spent on setting up, while the first night finds the house filled with family. And friends. Christine and Patrick stop over. I need to take this small break before I lock myself in the basement for three weeks. So much for focus.

Christine and I have so much catching up to do. I need to hear all about her engagement. She wants to know what went on with the show. I've got to tell her about Asher. She has to tell me about her wedding plans thus far. We've hidden ourselves, head-to-head, in the corner catching up, when the moment I've been dreading finally happens.

"So, I know you don't want to talk shop tonight, but I'm dying. Please show me my wedding gown! I need to see it in person. I mean the drawing in person. I know how much I loved it over Skype, but I bet I'll love it even more up close! I know you can't even think about it until after the show's done, but I can't wait anymore!"

Christine's not the impatient one. Heck, it took her almost a year to finally go out on a date with Patrick. So, if she's chomping at the bit about something, then I know it's a big deal for her.

What do I do?

If I show it to her, I know she's going to love it and want it. How do I tell her that the duchess may be wearing the same dress? I can't do that to her.

Reluctantly, I head to my room to get out my sketchbook. Even Kira doesn't know my dilemma. No one does.

I am weak and I'm a sucky friend. Christine deserves so much better than me. I feel like I'm a bad movie cliché, giving the promised thing away for fortune and fame.

So, I do what I have to do in this situation: I stall.

I come back out empty handed. "Oh, that's still packed. I haven't come across it yet." I think I'm a fairly decent liar. It's always worked with my parents. And most of the men in my life. I try to divert the conversation. "Speaking of aisles, where is it going to be? Are you doing The State Room? Or would it be too weird having it at the place you work? Inside? Outside? Do you even have a date? That'll impact your colors and flowers and all that."

Christine steps back and looks at me like I have three heads. Or maybe it's that my nose is growing like Pinocchio. "Why are you stalling? I want to see my dress."

"Sheesh, I wouldn't have pegged you for a bridezilla." I march back to the room with her close on my heels. Of course, my book is lying on top of my bed, in plain sight.

"Ha! I knew it! I want to see the dress."

Reluctantly, I flip to the page and hand her the book.

And then I watch her. Her face goes all soft and gooey and dreamy. Tears form in the corners of her eyes and begin to trickle down her face. She's in love.

Mother pucker. Of course she loves it. Because, well, it's the perfect look for her. Do I tell her about the duchess? I know my friend. She'll want me to win the show. She'll tell me to use her dress. I can't do that to her.

"It's even better than I'd imagined. I can't believe how perfect you made it. My whole life, all I've ever wanted was lace. I love lace. And this—it's enough detail without being over the top. The back is incredible. It's what I've always wanted." She whips out her phone and snaps a picture. Before I can stop her, she's sent it to her mom. "My mom's going to love it too. She's already tried to talk me out of a big poofy gown. I told her that you had it covered, and that you wouldn't let me down."

I have to tell her. That someone else will be wearing her dress first. She'll understand.

Who am I kidding? Only a truly horrible person would do that.

She's flipped to the next page with the bridesmaids' dresses. "I sort of like the idea of pink with the green. How did you know that that's what I'd pick?"

She's off on colors and flowers and time of year. She's thinking next May, so we've got time. At least, I've got time to hopefully get over being the world's worst friend.

****

"You have to actually start this assignment. I'm not here to watch you stare off into space all day."

Kira's tone is firm. Maybe a little harsh, but it's what I need, like a focus coach.

No matter how much I rub my eyes, they still feel like they're full of sand. Perhaps it's because I keep rubbing them. More likely it's due to the fact that I didn't actually sleep much last night.

"I guess we should get started."

"That would be smart." Kira's sarcastic, but in a good way.

"I think we're going to start with the groom's tuxedo first. For me, it's going to be the most challenging, so I'd rather get it out of the way."

"Oh, okay. Not at all how I thought you'd go, but tell me what you're thinking."

"So the deal is that when we come up with our color palettes, we let the producers know. They'll, in turn, let the event coordinators know for flowers and all. I'm not sure how they think they'll be pulling this together on such short notice."

"Yeah, I can't imagine the logistics."

"Neither can I. My best friend works at a facility that does weddings, and she's the main planner, so I sort of know what goes into it." Thinking of Christine makes me overwhelmed with guilt for a moment. Ugh. My stomach churns and my eyes continue to burn. I've got to focus. "So, here's what I'm thinking. The men's looks will be in navy. Just a skosh toward the royal, so it's more blue than dark. With cream and very light tan for shirts, vests, and ties. Then, I'm thinking a light blue, almost to periwinkle, but not quite, for the women. Perhaps with the navy accents. I'm kind of in love with this whole palette."

"And the wedding gown?"

"Ivory." And as I say it, I know it's got to be ivory. It works with the whole look. I can see flowers in whites and creams, with bursting blue hydrangeas and darker blue anemones and purplish blue veronicas. Even, if they got creative, even blueberries could be used for accents. Hastily, I scribble this down, the ideas flowing faster than I can write.

"Why blue?"

"Think about it. The whole set was blue. Any time we saw the duchess in her own clothes, they were blue. The Montabagan flag is blue. I think it's a national thing."

"Oh, that makes sense. And it's a detail that hopefully Fink won't pick up on."

"That's my hope."

The rest of the day flies by, fueled by coffee and adrenaline. It's only when I'm in my room, trying to go to sleep, that my moral battle continues to wage.

I want to win this show. But now I have to ask myself, at what cost?

Chapter 29

"It's been five days. We only have fifteen left." Kira's tapping her foot impatiently, twirling a piece of purple hair around her finger. "When are you going to show me already?"

How 'bout never?

"I'm still processing. When we get through all these." I wave to the pile of blue chiffon and organza. We've got the groomsmen's outfits and ring bearer done. The groom's tux is about seventy-five percent finished. Kira's working on it. I'm starting on the bridesmaids today. I've got them all designed and sketched out. Between the two of us, I figure we can knock the four dresses and flower girl dress in three days. I went off plan a bit and got three different shades of blue. Two dresses will be the same darkest shade, with different designs. There are two other shades that will be unique designs as well. The flower girl will be in a pale ivory with all three blues woven into her sash and trim.

"Are you sure about doing all the unique styles?" Kira's squinting at the scratch on my pages.

"I think. I mean, look at the measurements again. You've got the buxom one, the statuesque one, the petite one, and this girl looks like she may have some junk in her trunk. No one style's going to look great on all of them, and I simply love the way these colors work together. Especially with how I hope the flowers will be." I pull up the Pinterest pages with flowers and hold them next to the fabric.

Slowly, Kira nods. She's still twirling her hair. I can't look at it too long. When I met her it was green. Now it's multicolored. All these fantastic dark jewel tones set in black hair. Teal, purple, blue, green. I mean this in the nicest possible way when I say that she reminds me of the coloring of a rooster I'd seen in a 4-H exhibit at a county fair years ago. I would love to make a dress with fabric that looks like Kira's hair.

"Earth to Michele. Come in Michele."

I snap out of my rooster daydream and try to focus on what she's saying. Or said, because I'm pretty sure I missed it. "I'm sorry. It was your hair."

"Again?"

I blush. "Again. When this is all done and we can breathe again, we're going to have a long talk about how you did that. So, what were you saying?"

"I said that you may be right about the bridesmaids. It's sort of risky because it's not traditional, but it's not cray either."

"I hope."

I pull out the denim blue fabric to iron so I can start laying it out. If I had more time, I'd make a muslin pattern first. But with the volume of work, it's impossible. The bridesmaids' dresses are getting draped and pinned and made that way. I'll do a pattern for Maryn's dress. Whenever I decide what I'm doing with that.

Day bleeds into night. It's not the only thing bleeding. I've stuck most of my fingers at least once, with the exception of my left thumb, which could double as a pin cushion. It's only day six.

Oh crap, it's day six. Fourteen days. Two weeks.

It makes me want to cry. A lot. Or maybe it's the fatigue. We've been at this for almost a week. We're only a third of the way in. We're a third of the way done, if you consider the men a third, the girls a third, and the bride the last part.

But I think that's going to be more like half. I'd like ten days to make Maryn's gown. We're on pace to get that.

On the other hand, I want to sleep for days. I want to cry. I want to soak for four hours in a hot tub. I never want to see another cup of coffee again. I glance at Kira, hard at work on the flower girl's dress. She's making fabric covered buttons to trail down the back of the dress. All the bridesmaids' dresses have that too, as well as a decorative button somewhere. Because, well, buttons. They're my trademark and have been on every look thus far. I even put a subtle one on the bralette for the wedding night assignment.

"If I never have to make another fabric covered button again, it will be too soon," Kira says through gritted teeth. I feel very sorry for her. She's working probably as hard as I am. And she's not getting anything out of this. It's got to be hard to be this driven for no reward. I would have an issue if the roles were reversed.

Actually, maybe I wouldn't. I like to help my friends. I like to sew. Win-win, right? But still, this is sort of a crappy three weeks. Like the hardest ever.

We finish the attendants' looks about seven o'clock on the night of the ninth day. It means we're one day ahead of schedule, which makes me nervous. Like things are coming together too easily. And that can only mean that things will go disastrously wrong when I start the wedding gown.

"Okay, spill. What's the deal with the dress?" Kira and I are stretched out on the couches in the living room. Mom and Dad are over at Aunt Rosalie's for bridge night. Yes, I have parents who still play bridge. Actually, I think they end up playing blackjack and poker more than bridge, but they're trying not to sound like bad influences for their kids.

I take a sip out of my wine, which ends up being more like a chug as I drain my glass.

"You can't avoid this. We're getting started in the morning. We have to at least get fabric. We really have to do more than that, but I'm a little afraid that you've got nothing."

"That's the problem. I've got something. But it's not the right something."

"Are you drunk? Because that makes no sense."

I recount the story of the sketchbook and my moral quandary about my best friend's dream dress.

"Dude, that sucks."

"I know, right?" I want to refill my wine, but the bottle is like all the way across the room, and I don't have the strength to get up. Not to mention I probably can't afford to be hungover tomorrow.

"So, what are you doing?"

"I still don't know. I can give Maryn the dress she wants, thereby betraying my best friend. I can give my best friend the dress she wants, thereby disappointing Maryn, and most likely guaranteeing a loss. And the thing is, Christine's dress isn't right for

211

Maryn. It's not the right cut or silhouette. I can tweak it so it looks good, but it's not what she needs. On the other hand, what would be killer on her isn't what she thinks she wants. But if she sees the dress that's right for her, and it's not what she's expecting, will she even try it on? I know what she needs, and it's not Christine's dress. However, what if this isn't really about what she needs but what she wants? And what she wants is Christine's dress. I'm so confused."

"Understandable."

"And, if I give Maryn the dress, then how can I give it to Christine? It won't be special or unique. Everyone will think she's in a knock off. I can try and come up with something similar, but nothing will ever be as perfect for her. And she's my best friend. I don't want to give her sloppy seconds."

"But if you don't give the dress to Maryn ..."

"I'll lose."

"Can you deal with that?"

I really need more wine. "I don't know."

Chapter 30

Every single part of my body hurts. Even my eyelashes. I thought my time on the show was bad. This—this has been even worse. Trying to stay focused and motivated when there was a constant flurry of activity upstairs tested my every last nerve. Mom and the aunts, bless them, didn't understand that a day for Kira and me wasn't nine to five. We weren't going to stop for three square meals a day. Now I know why the producers made us take breaks to eat.

We lost plenty of time the day the film crew came by to do an update. They'd already been to see Fink, who lives in the city. I was next, and then they were on their way to see Asher.

I sort of miss him. In those thirty seconds daily when my brain was not consumed by thoughts of weddings, I think about him. And his offer.

With each passing day in my parents' house, it becomes more and more apparent that I don't belong here anymore. As much as I love my family, they seem stifling. I didn't have much time to think about it, but now that my creations—my masterpieces—are turned in, I will. I'm ready to leave home. That's why Asher's offer seems right, right now.

Kira and I finished one day early. My mom responded in typical fashion by having everyone over.

It's a nice thought certainly, but all I want to do is sleep. For three years.

I'm sorry we didn't finish even earlier, because I know how much Kira wanted to go home for a quick visit before we report to tape the finale. She has a five-year-old daughter. I can't imagine how hard it is to be away from her all this time. She misses her kid and husband tons. I'm not sure how she left them for this long. I'm so glad I picked Kira, not only because she was a machine, but because she's completely awesome. I feel totally geeky saying it, but even if I don't win, Kira's friendship is prize enough.

I'm standing in the kitchen—where else?—because if I sit down, I'll fall asleep. Kira's already retired, although I don't know how she can sleep with all these people in the house. Oh wait, I know. It's because we're dead tired.

A sidelong glance at the microwave tells me it's only seven-thirty. How much longer until these people leave? Tears threaten and then spring forth. I just want to go to sleep. I can't even process who's in the room or follow a conversation. I hear more commotion out in the living room, but couldn't care less. No one's even noticed I'm standing here crying.

"Hey there!"

It takes herculean strength to lift my head to see who's talking to me. "Tony. Lincoln. What are you doing here?" My voice is flat and dull. I wish there was some excitement in my voice, because it's good to see them. It is.

"We came to take you down to the city tomorrow."

"Oh. The show's sending a car."

"Okay, we were here for the weekend and were actually hoping we could hitch a ride down with you. Linc said you'd have a fancy car. Shame for you not to share it with your favorite cousin." Tony's grinning at me.

"I'd be happy to share it with my favorite cousin, but I don't think Carmalina wants to come to the city tomorrow. She's due in court." For the record, Carmalina is a high-powered attorney up here, not a criminal. Aunt Rosalie never lets me forget how successful she is.

"Ouch, that's rough. Just remember who lets you crash with them when you come to the city." Tony elbows me in the ribs. That doesn't help my "everything hurts" situation.

"Okay, you're right. Lincoln, you can ride in the car with me." I smile as he winks at me. Well, I do the best I can to smile. I'm afraid it comes out more like a demented grimace. That thought makes me start to laugh, which then, for some reasons, triggers the tears to flow in earnest rather than to just leak out of my eyes.

"Red alert, red alert. Tears. A-oogah. A-oogah." Tony's cupping his hands over his mouth, amplifying the noise of a tugboat. Have I mentioned how incredibly sensitive the men in my family are?

"Michele, are you okay?" At least Lincoln is showing his concern.

I try to nod yes, but it ends up with me shaking my head. I want to answer but all I can do is pinch my lips together in an ugly-quivery line.

Tony's looking at me like I've sprouted an extra head with hemorrhoids. I'm guessing Lincoln's equally horrified, but he does a better job masking it. "You wanna go talk somewhere?"

This time, I'm successful in nodding and am able to leave my perch by the kitchen sink. I walk down to my room with Lincoln close behind. Once in the room, I collapse on my bed and immediately retract into a fetal position. I can feel Lincoln pause for a minute, standing by the bed. "Um, do you mind?"

I can't see him but imagine he's pointing toward the bed. I shift over making room for him. I sold my queen-size bed when I gave up my apartment, and am relegated back to the twin-size bed of my youth. It's usually fine for me since I'm on the smaller side. Add Lincoln's newly filled-out frame, and the bed is quite full. Somehow, I don't seem to mind. Not at all.

"You know, every time I walk into Aunt Anne's house, you're a mess in front of the kitchen sink." It's sort of adorable that he calls my mom 'aunt.'

"I think it's more that I'm a mess."

"I know we can't blame this on Little Joey, so what's the issue tonight?"

Sniffling, I say, "Who says there's an issue?" *Sniff. Sniff.*

"Your face. And, I may be a dumb guy, but the tears are usually a good place to start. What happened?"

"This show happened."

"Aren't you pretty much done? I thought you got done early. That's what we're all here celebrating."

"Yeah, but I drove myself hard. Harder than I ever have. And I think ... I don't know. It's stupid."

"There are no stupid thoughts. Only stupid people."

"Gee, thanks." At least the tears have stopped, and I'm even smiling. A little.

I don't even know how to put into words what's going through my mind. There's so much, and it's all bombarding me. And I'm too tired to even begin to process it.

We lay there in silence. Lincoln being near me is helping. At least I'm calmer. My eyes are closed yet sleep seems a long way away.

"Lincoln?" My voice comes out small.

"Present."

"Are you happy?"

"Oh crap, we're getting deep now? I just thought you were a vulnerable chick, and I'd be able to cop a feel."

I elbow him. "Seriously."

"I am serious. You turned out hot for an old broad."

His delivery makes me laugh. "Well, I feel old. Yet, I feel young too. But I know I'm not anymore. That doesn't seem to matter, since I'm no closer to having my life together. Actually, I feel like it's more of a mess. Like I'm floating out in space with no hope of ever finding gravity."

"That's got to be scary."

"It is. Have you ever felt like that?"

"Maybe a little. Toward the end of college. I wasn't sure what exactly I was going to do—whether to take a year off, go right to grad school, where to go to grad school, what to focus on. That sort of thing."

"But that's all responsible stuff. I'm not responsible."

"Why not?"

I think about that long and hard. "Because it's not easy. I like to take the easy way out."

"And how's that working for you?"

"Um, it's not."

"So what are you going to do?"

"I don't know. That's the problem. And I'm so tired and burnt out. And I want this so bad, but I don't know. This was so hard."

"So was this show the easy way out?"

Again, I have to stop to think about it. "I thought it was. I thought it'd be fun and I'd get to sew, and then maybe I'd be famous and win lots of money."

"But that's not what happened, was it?"

"No, it was work. Lots of work. Probably more work than I've ever done in my life. Like, combined. And I missed my family. And some people were mean. And it challenged me like I've never been challenged. And that was good, but it was hard."

"Things can be good and hard."

Those words hang in the air like some obscene cartoon bubble. As much as I want to be mature, I can't. The giggles start. The more I try not to giggle, the harder my body convulses with laughter.

"Nice. You know what I mean."

"I like things good and hard. Just not at the moment. My whole family is here."

Now Lincoln's laughing too. The whole bed is shaking. And making a noise that could easily be mistaken for other activity.

"Shhhh. Stop. This bed is squeaky. We're going to get in trouble." I can't stop laughing either, and at least now the tears are from laughter instead of fatigue.

After a few minutes, I'm able to breathe somewhat normally. Lincoln's relaxed, lying on his back next to me. We're shoulder to shoulder, hip to hip, but only because this is a freakishly small bed. It's odd, because although we're not intentionally touching, it's incredibly intimate all at the same time.

"Do you feel better?"

"I'm still dead tired and worn out, but thanks. I needed that."

"I'm glad to be of service, although normally when I'm in bed with someone, I don't want them laughing uncontrollably at me."

"Yeah, but it's not like we're *in bed* in bed. We're on bed. Totally different."

He's quiet for a minute. "Yeah. Right."

"Okay, let me ask you this. How do you come up with a plan?"

"So we're back to that. You change subjects so fast that I could get whiplash."

"I didn't change the subject, I got back on it after you derailed it."

"Sure."

I feel my eyes growing heavy and my body going limp. I hope he tells me the secret to long-term planning before I fall asleep. "No really. Even though you're younger than me, in life skills, you're like way older. How do I get it together?"

"Thanks, I think. Anyway, to come up with a plan, first you need to figure out what you want. What's the end goal? Until you do that, it's pretty hard to figure out a way to get there. Otherwise, you don't know where you're going and you wander around aimlessly."

"I think I've got that down pat." I cannot hold back the enormous yawn that ruptures from my mouth. "Lincoln, this has been good. Really good. But I need to sleep. For about a year."

The bed depresses and then lightens. He bends over and gives me a warm kiss on the forehead. "Get some rest."

"Thanks." Another yawn. "When did you get so smart and grown up?" He smiles and quietly leaves the room. I feel cold and lonely without him lying there next to me. I should have asked him to stay until I fell asleep.

But that would be weird, wouldn't it?

For some reason, I don't think it would.

Chapter 31

I swear to God, Tony's hitting on Kira. We're in the car, heading back to New York City for the finals, and Tony's putting the full-court press on her. Does he not notice the ring on her finger?

I mean, it's sort of cute. She's about ten years older than he is, but seeing her blush when he compliments her is charming. It's not my job to tell Tony she's married to some big burly lumberjack guy who could probably kick his butt into next week. Tony would sort of deserve it, moving in on another man's territory. Not that women are property, but Tony should at least respect her vows. He was raised better than that.

I glance across at Lincoln, who's watching this with as much amusement as I am. Lincoln truly has turned out nicely. I sit back and smile proudly, as if I had anything to do with it. Tony and Lincoln are good guys. Even when Tony doesn't know his boundaries. On the other hand, what's the harm with a little flirting? I mean I was sort of doing that with Lincoln last night, even though I'm sort of involved with Asher.

Funny. I haven't thought about him that much. Okay, I have, but not to my normal degree of obsession. I've wondered how he was doing with his pieces, and how much competition he'd be. I'm pretty worried about that. Most of my recent Asher-related thoughts have definitely centered around the show. Huh. Normally I would be concerned that I wasn't that into him, but this is not a normal time. The show really has consumed most of my waking moments in addition to a fair amount of sleeping ones as well. Man, some of the dreams I've had ... but I digress.

Before I can start ruminating or obsessing about my lack of obsessing, we're at the studio building. My pieces were packed in a van that followed the car down. Kira and I've got to bring the clothing rack up to the studio. I'm not sure how this is going to work.

We bid Lincoln and Tony a farewell, and I promise to call or text as soon as I have news.

Oh God, this is getting real. My breath starts coming rapidly. It's hard to get air into my lungs. Oh no.

"So, what's the deal with Tony? He's a cutie."

I don't know if Kira is really interested, or if she sees me about to freak out. I don't care. I'm simply happy for the distraction.

"Aren't you married?"

"Yeah, but I'm not dead. I can still look. And he's not so bad to look at."

"Eeew. That's gross."

"Gross? Why?"

"He's my cousin, but he's more like a brother. I certainly like him more than I like my brothers. I mean, that's probably because I don't like their wives and the men they turn into when they're around their spouses. Tony doesn't have that sort of baggage. He's a kid."

"He doesn't look like a kid to me." The way she says it is a little dirty sounding. Eeew again.

"He's only like twenty-five."

"That'd be fun. It's not like I'm looking. All I'm saying is that it could be fun."

I crinkle my nose. "Twenty-five is young. They're immature." The ridiculousness of that statement hits me. "Well, I mean, Lincoln's actually fairly mature. Like, he was sort of giving me advice on how to get my life together. Apparently, I need to come up with a plan or something."

"Yeah, what's going on with you two? I thought you were dabbling with Asher. And I know you're vanilla, so you're not the type to do a two-fer, are you?"

"A what? No. It's—there's nothing. Lincoln and I are friends. He's like Tony. Like my brother."

"Are you sure?"

"Well, yeah. I mean, I'm seriously considering moving to London with Asher. I think maybe that's where I might make my plan. I can't maybe think about the fact that I might go with Asher if I'm interested in Lincoln."

"That certainly clears that up."

"I ... uh ..." I don't get to finish. The elevator has arrived at our floor. The doors open.

It's go time.

****

I lean over and whisper. "But I still don't understand. If the show airs, then they're going to know what she's wearing. If it waits until after the wedding, then the audience will know who won. How is this going to work?"

Asher shrugs. "I'm sure they've got it all figured out. They'll let us know. Relax."

"I can't relax. I've only had one night of relaxing this whole time." I don't mention that it was last night and that it happened because Lincoln helped.

"Is that because you were missing me so much?" Ash has that damn cocky grin on his face that can do all sorts of things to a woman's parts. And probably some men's parts too.

"Sure. That was it. I was prostrate with grief every night because you weren't in my bed."

I do feel a small twinge of guilt that I wasn't missing Asher in that way. I was thinking about him, certainly, but in the competition sense. It will be interesting to see where things go and how they progress when the weight of the competition isn't bearing down.

I don't have time to feel too guilty, thank goodness, because Katy, the head producer, begins talking. "Okay peeps, here's how it's going to shake down. We tried to fly the wedding party over to try on their garments, but it's going to be too hectic. We've found models that approximate the sizes but know that the fit may not be perfect. The duchess will be trying on each look to decide. In terms of the show and taping, we're going to show the runway for the wedding party. We will not be showing any of the bridal looks, in the interest of maintaining that surprise. But here in studio we'll get to see the duchess model each look."

So that's how they're going to do it.

Katy continues. "Tonight, we'll be announcing a winner. That will all be filmed, along with the duchess' reaction and comments on each gown. Following tonight's taping, the winner will board a plane and fly to the United Republic of Montabago where *he*—or she—will begin work on alterations and final details. *He*—or she—will also be a guest at the royal wedding!"

I don't like the way Katy keeps putting the emphasis on *he*. Like she already knows who's going to win. She probably does, and that slip of the tongue told me all I needed to know. Asher for the win.

I should have expected it, with everything that happened with the gown. I guess I hoped I'd made the right decision after all. Apparently, I did not.

It's hard to keep my spirits up as we wait for the models to emerge. I haven't spoken to Fink, and I feel no real need to. Her look is first.

She chose black. Black bridesmaids' dresses, black tuxes. Black upon black upon black. With fire engine red flowers. Her dresses—all the same, mind you—don't look bad per se. Again, I contend that it's hard to get a one-look-flatters-all when the sizes and shapes are that varied. It's a meh wedding party at best, in terms of royal weddings.

Then Maryn emerges in the dress. Oh gosh, it's terrible. I mean, the dress is most likely well constructed, but no. Just no. First of all, it's strapless. This is a royal wedding. There's an exorbitant amount of crystal and beading on the front, from the plunging sweetheart neckline down to the princess waistline, which is also outlined in crystals and beading. The effect of the beaded top and waist is to cut Maryn off and make her look short. That's only magnified by the enormous ball gown skirt that envelops and overwhelms her. There's more lace and beading scrolling up and down the bottom of the massive skirt, which makes it look (and probably feel) heavy. Fink's added a heavy looking crystal headpiece and thick frothy veil. It's hard to see Maryn under all that meringue. How Maryn is overwhelmed by the dress— well, it's a petite girl's biggest fear. One of the main reasons why I make most of my own clothes. It's simply all wrong.

I feel bad for her. I should feel bad for Fink, but, well, I don't. I glance over at her, and she's beaming proudly. Not a care in the world. I guess there's no accounting for taste.

The judges' critique expresses what I'd been thinking, and now disappointment is starting to register with Fink. The stage clears and then we wait. It's down to Asher and me.

I think I'm going to throw up.

Chapter 32

I have every right to be scared out of my mind. Asher's designs are immaculate. The men's suits, even on the models, look like they were crafted by the angels. I want to run my fingers over the fabric and seams. Flawless, as to be expected. His female bridal attendants are all in a very soft pink. Flowing chiffon that looks more liquid than solid. The dresses are the same cut, but with the empire waist, he's managed to make most of them look very beautiful. I'd wear those dresses and not even complain.

Then Maryn comes out, and perhaps I feel a little choked up. Not full tears, but there's certainly emotion. Her dress is white. It's also empire waist. Here's the thing—all the experts will tell you that an empire waist is great for a petite woman, as it gives the illusion of a longer leg. And I get that. But when I look at empire waists, all I think is, "Is she carrying a bump under there?"

Anywho. That's neither here nor there, because Maryn looks beautiful. The lace capped sleeves, the cut out in the upper back, framed by the lace. It gives the illusion of being sexy while still being modest. The dress only has a small little train, more of a puddle at the back. However, Asher used an impossibly light cathedral-length veil that follows her like a wispy cloud, and gives the regal effect of a train. He's used pearl beading around the waist and on the lace upper body, as well as to dot the veil. She's wearing simple, yet elegant, pearl earrings and a bracelet. The styling is perfect for this look.

Callie Smalls reads the critique. She herself is in an understated taupe suit with a fascinator, as if she's already in attendance at the wedding. F.Y.I., taupe is not a good color on her. "This gown is impeccable. While it does not have the volume of a more traditional wedding gown, the duchess appreciates the lightness and ease of wear. She says that she could easily imagine spending her wedding day wearing this dress!"

Well, there it is. They might as well not even show mine. Asher's got it. Who doesn't want to feel comfortable when they're all dressed up?

I put my head between my knees to wait for my look. I just want this to be over. How am I ever going to be gracious on camera? How will I not resent Asher? I can't resent him. He did a better job. That's all there is to it. He gave the duchess what she wanted, even if she didn't know it.

I take a sip of water as they announce my collection. As the wedding party makes its entrance, I lose my breath. The multiple hues of blue are stunning together. It's definitely a more edgy look, but I'm in love with it. Love. And now, the moment of truth. I see her silhouette behind the screens. Oh God, I can't breathe.

Duchess Maryn emerges, looking everything like the princess she's about to become. I can't help myself—I start to cry. She's breathtaking. I'm sure it's because she's wearing my dress but ... no, she just looks that good.

The ivory satin is perfect with her skin tone. The chiffon that wraps around her arms to form the off-the-shoulder neckline is classic and elegant. Just the tips of her shoulders and collarbones show. A hint of something more to come, yet modest enough for church. The bodice is fitted, showing off her bust, with a slight rouching that gathers to the side where the buttons march down her flank, rather than down the back. It's a new twist on an old style, updating the look. The waist is slightly dropped, then flares out into an A-line skirt. Chiffon floats in gathers and soft layers over the silk skirt. A small bow adds a detail to the waist. The train trails behind, completing the regal look. The look is somewhat reminiscent of Grace Kelly, but different at the same time. A small pearl tiara sets off a full blusher-length veil.

Maryn looks tall and regal and well, stunning. I can't help the tears and the smiles. Even if I don't win, I know I made the right choice. This dress, this is what she was meant to wear on her wedding day.

Then I notice it. There's not a sound in the studio, save the hum of the lights. I glance around. I'm not the only one crying. I hope the other tears are because of how insanely gorgeous she looks and not because they think she looks ridiculous.

Callie Smalls, looking ridiculous next to the elegant duchess, steps up onto the runway. "This was not the look that Duchess Maryn had been expecting from Michele, which was initially disappointing."

Oh crap.

"That is, until the duchess slipped into this perfect creation. While satin may sometimes feel heavy, balanced by the chiffon, it doesn't weigh her down. As she has all season, Michele got the fit and proportions exactly right. Having the classic bridal buttons on the side of the dress gives it something new and edgy, while still playing on a traditional element. The off-the-shoulder neckline exposes the perfect amount of skin for a wedding in a cathedral. Modest but modern. It brings to mind an era of royalty and glamour while being something that every modern bride dreams of possessing."

Okay. I can live with that.

Maryn exits the runway, and they begin the final preparations for the announcement. Before I can even blink, Asher's in front of me, enveloping me into a large hug. "Michele, that was stunning. You blew me away. Damn it. I should have known."

As he sets me down I say, "Should have known what?"

"That you'd blow me out of the water. I cannot keep up with you. Your mind is brilliant. That wedding gown—simply smashing."

I feel the heat fill my cheeks. I should probably learn how to take a compliment some day. "Uh, um ... well, your suits were gorgeous. That was so hard for me. And your gown was beautiful too."

"I thought so until I saw yours. You nailed it. Bloody hell, everyone in the place was crying."

"Yeah, but it's not what she wanted. She wanted a different design that I'd done. But I, well, I couldn't give it to her."

"Why not? You always give a client what they ask for. First rule of business."

"I thought it was that the customer is always right."

"Same difference. You've got this in the bag."

"I wouldn't say that. She really liked how easy and comfortable your dress was. Wedding days are long. Comfort is important."

"No, not for this. She should totally sacrifice comfort for fashion to be in your dress. Plus, knowing how thorough you are, you've made it as comfortable as it can be."

I look down at my feet and hope the blush isn't as apparent as I think it is. "I know that my wish is to wear a dress without having to wear major scaffolding underneath it. Do you know how hard it is to pull Spanx up and down when you've had your nails done or had too much to drink? God forbid, both? I tried to build the support into the dress so she doesn't have to have all that on underneath."

"You built the bra into the dress?"

"Of course. Strapless bras just fall down, especially when there's any heft to the breasts. I put the boning and cups right into the lining of the dress."

"Damn genius right there."

"Consider it insider information."

Asher opens his mouth to say more but is interrupted by Katy.

"Okay, places everyone. It's time to announce the winner."

Chapter 33

I must be humble. I must be gracious. I must be calm.

Who the heck am I kidding?

I WON!!!!

The idea of passing out runs through my mind when Callie Smalls announces that in just over two weeks, Duchess Maryn Medrovovich will be wearing an original, one-of-a-kind design by Michele Nowakowski.

Instead, my mouth drops open, too stunned to speak. Asher again crushes me to him, cutting off my airflow a little. No biggie. Before I know it, I'm swarmed by all the contestants. I find Kira and smush her into a hug. "We did it!"

"No, you did it! I'm so proud!"

"No, *we* did it. There's no way I would have gotten through without you. You kept me focused, and that alone deserves a prize!"

"Truth."

Our arms are around each other and we're jumping up and down, squealing like little girls. I can't wait to call my parents and Lynn and Lincoln and Tony and Christine to tell them.

Some bottles of champagne appear and uncorked. While I dream of shaking the bottles and spraying them all over the set like athletes celebrating in a locker room, I expect that I'm supposed to be more dignified than that. But let's face it, this is my World Series and Super Bowl all rolled into one. Not only did I win this contest, which is super awesome in and of itself, but my dress is going to be seen around the world.

This is life changing.

It's getting a little hard to breathe. Oh gosh, I may really pass out now. Breathe in, breathe out. Don't think about the loss of privacy, the critics, the pressure. Just ...

****

"I think she's coming to. Give her some room to breathe." The voice is far away, but I know they're referring to me.

My head hurts. My pride hurts more. Please, God, let the cameras not have captured that on tape.

"Should we start rolling again? We can get her coming out of it, to splice in with the footage of her going down."

Guess that prayer's not getting answered today.

It doesn't matter. I won.

I may need some valium.

I struggle to sit up. There's a medic, but I push him away. "I'm fine."

"Ma'am, are you okay? What happened?"

The medic is cute, but I'm guessing he's not too bright if he can't figure out how I ended up down on the floor.

"I passed out." I try to keep the snarkiness out of my voice. "I think I had a bit of a panic attack or something. This is kind of overwhelming."

I look around and Kira and Asher are right there. I reach to them, and they help me upright. "It sort of hit me, you know. All of this. What it means."

Asher continues holding my hand. "This is big. You're going to be a household name."

"Yeah, that's what sort of sent me into a panic. I can't think about that now."

"You'll think about it tomorrow?" Kira chimes in.

"Huh? I guess. I mean, I don't want to think about it now, but I don't see how I can not think about it from this point forward."

She shakes her head, and smiles at Asher. "Kids today." He pats my head.

I look from one of them to the other. They obviously have some secret that I don't know about. "What? What are you talking about?"

Kira sighs. "It's a famous line from *Gone With the Wind.* You have heard of that, haven't you?"

"Obviously." I wrack my brain. It's a movie, I'm pretty sure. Like an old one. Okay, I'm fine. I get it. "So, I don't know old movies. Sue me."

A shocked look crosses Kira's face. "It's a book, and a movie. The movie won tons of Oscars. It's an epic classic. I am so making you read the book and then watch the movie."

Asher chimes in. "She's got at least an eight-hour flight to get to Montabago. That's about right."

"*Eight hours?* The movie is eight hours long? What the heck? Are you nuts? That's not a movie. That's like a whole season on Netflix!"

Kira rolls her eyes. "It's not eight hours long. Asher's trying to be funny. I mean, the book is sort of long, but it's soooo worth it. It's a quick read for eight hundred pages. The movie's only about four-and-a-half hours long. Not too bad."

"Eight hundred pages? I may pass out again! That's like the size of a dictionary. How do you expect me to read that? Maybe I can watch the movie, but no dice on the book. And—" something occurs to me "—why are we talking about this anyway? I just won *Made for Me*. I've got celebrating to do!"

Kira winks at Asher, and then looks at me. "Do you still feel panicked?"

I think about it for a second. "Not really. I mean, the thought of reading a book that long makes me want to hyperventilate, but I do feel better about all this." I look at the smile on Kira's face. "Thanks, friend."

The next few hours are a whirlwind, with the production interviews, thanking the crew, talking with the cast, and even a sit-down with the duchess.

I've had my champagne and have switched to water. The adrenaline is still coursing through my veins, although I expect a crash any minute. I know this because the minute I sit down, I realize my feet hurt. As do my legs. And my head, but I think that might be from the whole passing out thing.

Maryn, of course, looks so composed and together. I should try to be more like her. Which is laughable because I blurt out the first thing on my mind. "Are you mad that I didn't give you the other dress?"

She's a bit taken aback at my bluntness. Probably because I was a bumbling idiot the last time I talked to her. I don't think my bumbling idiotness status has changed; I'm simply more direct this time.

"Well, um, no, I can't say that I was mad. Disappointed? Yes. Of course, that ended the moment I put your gown on. After that, I was like, 'what other dress?'"

My breath expels involuntarily as I sink back into my chair. "I thought it was certain death not to give you the other dress, but I just couldn't."

"Why, may I ask? Why did you show it to me and then not make it for me?"

"That's the thing. It was in my sketchbook because I only have the one book. I don't have separate books for separate things. I use one book until it's full, and then start a new one. That design is for my best friend Christine. She's newly engaged. I drew that before I even knew about the engagement, but I had a feeling it was coming. And then, without seeing the drawing, she described to me what she thought she wanted, and it's pretty much that dress."

"So you wouldn't give me her dress?"

I nod. "Basically. I really struggled with it. I toyed with changing it a bit so it wasn't exactly the same. But that's not the only reason."

"Oh? Loyalty to a friend is not a good enough reason?"

"That was, and I'll admit I did consider selling out. But there's a reason why I couldn't."

"Do tell." The duchess has a posh polish to her, obviously. Her voice is sort of snooty, but I think it's just how she sounds. I don't think she's actually a snob. Not a total one at least.

"Christine—my best friend—is shaped totally different than you are. She's freakishly tall. Like Amazonian. And she's a ballet dancer, so her frame is different. Small bust. That other dress was designed for her. It would have been okay on you, but I thought that a royal wedding needed more than okay. And you deserved something made especially for you. I mean, isn't that the whole premise of the show?"

She smiles. "I appreciate your integrity. I thought the dress you drew was beautiful, but you're right. You understand my body."

It's my turn to smile. "I don't know if you've noticed, but we're about the same size. Your bust is a little bigger, though. I understand the struggle, and believe me, it's real."

"Plus, you seem to understand taste and decorum. What is appropriate and what is not."

"I come from a large, relatively conservative family. My mother won't let me wear shorts or jeans to church still, and she believes the shoulders should be covered in the house of our Lord. I'm not saying I'm as conservative as all that, but it's how I was raised."

"I agree. There's a level of conservatism that I've agreed to by entering into this marriage. There are some things that I would love to wear that my station does not permit. And now I sound like a stuck-up old snot talking about her station."

I smile and squeeze her hand. "I don't know if you know, but I passed out earlier."

"I'm aware. I was here."

"I had a panic attack thinking about how my life is going to change and all the responsibility and pressure that I'm going to have. I can't imagine how that must be for you. And since I'm going to be at your beck and call for the next year, let me know what you need and how I can help."

Maryn smiles again. "It's hard to have friends sometimes. That being said, I feel that I may have just made a new one."

Holy crap. I'm friends with a princess.

Chapter 34

"You won."

"I won."

Asher and I are standing there, awkwardly staring at each other. It's time to leave the studios and re-enter the real world. For him at least. For me, I've got about four days before I fly to Montabago and work on the wedding.

"What's your plan now? Do you head to California first or are you going right to London?"

"London. I've got a flat."

"Oh. How did you find it?"

"Craigslist."

"They have that over there?" I really need to study up on England if I'm going to not sound like a moron when I talk to Asher.

"I hope so, otherwise I'm going to be homeless."

"Bite your tongue." I playfully hit him on the arm. "Where is it?"

"It's in Spitalfields."

I nod. "Oh, okay. That's awesome."

He starts laughing. "You don't have any idea where that is, do you?"

"I'm not even sure where London is in the world."

"Oh, my dear. Please study up in your free time. There's so much to do and so much to see. I can't wait to show you, but it'll be better if you have some idea of what you're looking at."

"I'll try. I still need to figure out where exactly Montabago is."

Asher laughs again before pulling me into a hug. Resting his chin on my head, I hear him say, "I'm happy for you. If it couldn't be me, I'm glad it's you. We're going to conquer the fashion world together."

"So you still want me to join you when I'm done?"

"Of course. Why wouldn't I?"

"Is there room for me in your apartment?"

"Flat. It's a flat. And yes. Plenty of room. And we'll share studio space and resources. With your winnings, we'll be living it up."

That makes my spine go stiff. "What do you mean by that?" My voice is soft, and I'm not even sure he can hear me.

"Obviously, with your prize, we can afford much better space and equipment."

"Oh, right. Are we sharing equipment?"

"That only makes sense. And you'll be able to buy the top of the line! Don't worry. We'll have a smashing good time." With that, he kisses me. I don't know if he's trying to convince me or him.

It works.

All too soon his car pulls up. I don't want him to go. I'm sad, but there are no tears. That's odd for me. I'm probably torn in too many directions to cry at the moment. "I'll text you when I land. I'll start sending you pictures of the flat and our new neighborhood."

"I don't know if my phone will work when I'm in Europe. Try me through Facebook too. I'm not sure if I'll be able to call you, but if I can I will. I'm a little afraid for this wedding." It'll be weird be all connected to the world again.

"You'll be smashing, as always. Try not to stress."

"Have you met me?"

"Of course. That's why I'm giving you this advice. You got everything done in time. You won. She picked you for a reason. I'm sure you'll do fine."

He's off, the shiny black car pulling away. I know in a few days, I'll have a similar, if not the same, ride to the airport, where my life will change forever.

I'm heading to Lincoln and Tony's place tonight. I should go back to my parents' tomorrow and pack. Who knows when I'm coming back stateside, and I'll want more things than I have in my suitcase when I move to London.

I'm moving to London.

Holy crap.

I know nothing about London. Truth be told, I don't know all that much about Asher either. I mean, he's super hot. He went to boarding school. He's not close with his family. His sexual orientation is a lot more fluid than mine. He's already a successful designer and is trying to conquer the European market. I don't even know how old he is. He's got a sibling, but I couldn't tell you if it's a brother or sister. He rarely sees his parents.

I'm not sure we are super compatible. But you know what they say, opposites attract, so I'm sure we'll be fine. We have to be, right? I'm moving to another continent for him. It'll be fine. No, not fine. It'll be good. It's a plan, and it's been established that I need a plan. So now, I've got one. And it will be fine. Although I'm not sure what he meant about living it up because of my winnings. I've got to be smart—conservative—with my money this time around. No more credit card debt. Although I guess investing in some more equipment isn't a bad idea. But still, I'm not totally comfortable with that conversation. We'll definitely have to revisit it.

By the time I reach Lincoln and Tony's, my feet are killing me and I need a nap. I don't get how people walk around all the time like this. I'm sure I'd get used to it, if I lived here. That would be sort of cool, living here. There are so many interesting fabric shops in the garment district, not to mention the antique and eclectic buttons I could find. New York has this energy to it that really inspires me. I wonder if London has the same thing.

As I turn the key in the lock, I say a quick prayer that Slick Rick isn't there. I don't know that I have the energy to deal with him right now. You'd think the dude would get a clue.

"SURPRISE!!!!!"

Tony and Lincoln have decorated their place. Well, as much as two bachelors know how to do. There are about five balloons and a banner that says 'CONGRATULATIONS MICHELE!' They're there, along with my parents, Lynn, and Christine.

"How did you? The episode hasn't aired ... and I'm not supposed ..."

Lincoln steps forward. "Do you really think that I've been taking Lauren out all this time because I like her? She's got the personality of a sea urchin."

I'm not sure what kind of personalities sea urchins have because I've never met one, so I assume he means prickly, with which I concur. "You've been spying?"

"Of course. I'm too nosy not to."

"But I'm not supposed to be talking about this."

"As long as it doesn't make it to social media, you're fine."

My parents rush forward and swallow me up in a huge hug. My mom's crying. "We're so proud of you, baby. I kept telling your father that if we gave you the time to find yourself, it would all work out. And now it has! You're a winner!"

My dad, ever the optimist, chimes in. "Have you thought about what you're going to do after your commitment to the show ends? This is the time to capitalize on your fifteen minutes. You need to have a plan."

Lynn laughs. "Did you say 'Michele' and 'plan' in the same sentence? Michele has a lot of great strengths and more talent in her little finger than I have in my whole body, but planning is not one of them."

It's my turn. This is gonna knock their socks off. "Lynn's right. I'm not a planner. Except for this time. I've totally got it all figured out." Okay, this is my moment. I have to tell my family what I'm going to do. They're going to be so proud of me for putting this all together. I sit down on the couch and take a quick sip of champagne that Christine's handed me. I can do this.

Of course, trying to take a deep breath and swallow a sip of champagne are tasks that should not be attempted simultaneously. After coughing and sputtering for a few minutes, with tears rolling down my face (this time from pain, not for any other reason), I can finally start again. Oddly enough, I find I can't look at Lincoln while I say this.

"I've got a plan. I'm going to Europe—to Montabago—for a few weeks for the show. I've got to be there for the wedding and to make sure the bridal party fits well and all that. Then, after that's done, I'm going to London. I'm going to work from there. I have an internet-based business, so it doesn't really matter where in the world I am. I can sew anywhere."

My mom's looking a little pale. "London? Like England?"

"Yes, of course London, England. You know, trying something new. I've got space in an apart—I mean flat, and studio space. I'll run my Esty business from there. And, since my primary job for the year will be making clothes for the new princess, I'll be closer than if I were here. It'll be more convenient for fittings and consultations and all that."

For once, my mom is speechless. My dad's mouth is opening and closing like a trout, gasping for air. Lynn sinks down onto the arm of the couch, as if her legs have been turned to Jell-O.

"See? I have a plan. And it's a good one too."

Christine, who's usually quiet in relation to my family, is the first to speak. "Are you moving there to be with him?" I'd obviously told her a little about Asher when I was home. Not tons, because I didn't have that much time to visit. But she at least knows there's a guy.

I nod and smile. "Yeah. He's relocating there from California, trying to get a foot in the European market. We're going to share studio space."

"And living space?" That's from Lincoln. I give him a dirty look. I was going to try to gloss over that. I don't think my parents are going to be thrilled with the fact that we're cohabitating.

"Well, yes. We're both adults, and it's what we want."

That's enough to send pretty much everyone in the apartment into a tizzy.

"You've just met him!"

"We don't even know his parents!"

"What are you doing?"

"What are you thinking?"

"Are you nuts?"

"But I need you to be here to help me plan my wedding." I can barely hear Christine's voice above the din. Her words cut me the most. I do want to be here to plan her wedding.

"I'll still be able to help you plan it. That's what FaceTime and Skype are for. With the internet, we'll be in constant contact. And, I'll fly back here with your dress. Maybe you can even come to London for a fitting? How cool would that be?"

Lynn clears her throat. "But you can't hold a baby over the internet."

I feel my eyes grow wide as I turn to look at her. "A baby?"

My mom jumps up. "A BABY?"

Then there's more jumping and squealing and hugging.

A winner, a wedding, and a baby. This is, like, the best day ever.

Chapter 35

"So, London?"

"Yep. London. It makes sense, I think." Lincoln and I are sitting on the couch. The crowd has left, making the drive back Upstate. It was so nice of them to come down and surprise me. Tony's gone out on a late night pizza run to satiate my empty belly. Slick Rick is out of town on business. Thank goodness. Apparently he travels a lot, which is a good thing. I do not like that guy. Maybe I should fix him up with Fink.

"Why does London make sense?" We're both staring straight ahead, but are sitting close together. Very close together. Shoulder to shoulder, hip to hip again, like that night on my bed. Other people had been sitting on the couch with us, forcing us into this position. Even though we'd gotten up to say good-bye, we returned to where we'd been sitting. I like it though. Lincoln makes me feel more relaxed.

"Because I'll need to go to Montabago throughout the year anyway. And well, Asher."

Lincoln's quiet for a minute. A long minute.

"Have you thought this through?"

"Of course. You don't move across the world on a whim." Except that's sort of what I was doing.

"Have you thought about your finances? Do you already have a corporation set up? Are you going to reestablish as a European business? That's probably the best idea, unless of course you plan on moving back here. Then, you'll get hit with the re-patriation tax if you try to move your money here. At that point you'd probably be better off becoming a British citizen and not moving your money back here."

"So I could never come back?"

"Financially, it could be disastrous. Plus, we don't know the effect the Brexit will have on the economy, and it might be harder to sell to the E.U. once that goes into effect."

"I don't know what most of those words mean."

"Do you have a business plan?"

"Um, well, I sell things through my Etsy shop."

"But you're not going to continue that, are you? I mean, you need to incorporate. And probably get an L.L.C. so your personal assets are protected. The publicity of the show is going to propel you into the forefront. You're going to need help with the business aspect, the shipping, and probably even the actual sewing. Do you know what you're looking for?"

His words are assaulting me and making my brain hurt. So much for my plan. I really thought I'd thought this all through.

"I, um, well, I don't know a lot about business. I would need some help with that, I suppose. I guess I don't have a very business-oriented mind."

"Does this guy know a lot about business?"

"I don't know. I mean, I know Asher had his own company. He did have a partner, though I gather that guy was more of a designer than a business man. That's part of why Asher left. He wants to branch out into the European market." I pause for a minute. "So, I do think Asher has some business sense. He went to Columbia for his MBA. Maybe he'll be able to help me get my feet on the ground."

Lincoln's quiet for a minute. "What's your target market? Because if you two have the same market, then you're competitors. Why should he help his competition become more successful?"

"I don't think that will be an issue. My customers, I think, will be American, and he's looking to expand into Europe more."

"Okay, well, I guess that's good, but you're going to get murdered on shipping charges."

We sit there in silence. Lincoln's certainly given me a lot to think about. Maybe before I relaunch my store, I'm going to have to take some time to get all this figured out. While learning a new continent. And starting a new relationship. And a new job as the private seamstress—no, fashion designer—to a princess. Whoa. That's a lot to handle. I don't think I can do it. My mind is whirring. There's no way. I'm about to freak out. Yet again.

Finally, still sitting side by side, virtually motionless, Lincoln speaks. "Are you okay?"

I swallow, but the rock in my throat doesn't want to go down. "I don't think so. There's so much. It's so overwhelming."

"Yes, it can be. It can also be fun and exciting. The key is to stay focused and organized."

I turn to look at him. "Have you met me? That's not something I'm good at."

His blue eyes twinkle as he smiles. "I have met you. That's why I'm telling you all this ahead of time.

So you can start figuring it out, even if it's just hiring people to handle it for you."

When he says that, a rush of relief runs through my body. "You mean I can do that? I don't have to do it alone?"

"Of course not. There's no way you can. But you do have to educate yourself and surround yourself with knowledgeable, trustworthy people."

I'm very uneasy with the direction of this conversation. And I've hit my maximum for being able to sit still. Pacing will make me feel better.

But it doesn't and I find myself standing in the middle of the living room, looking at Lincoln, who is still sitting on the couch. How can he be still for that long?

He's watching me. And suddenly, I'm mad. Mad at him for doubting me. Mad that I hadn't thought of these points and that I don't have answers. Mad that I know he's right and that I probably can't do this. But all that matters is that I'm mad.

"You know, screw you! Screw you and your taxes and business plans and all that! Everyone wants to know why I don't do anything. Why I'm not successful. Well, I'll tell you why! Because no one believes in me. No one supports me. No one just says, 'atta girl, we knew you could do it.' Everyone always criticizes me. Tells me all the things I *can't* do. And I'm sick of it!"

Of course, this is all malarkey. My family is supportive. I'm the reason that I'm thirty and homeless and without a job. I've never worked hard enough or stayed focused enough for long enough to accomplish anything. Ain't no way in hell I'm admitting that to Lincoln though. It's easier to get mad at him.

"I didn't tell you you *can't* do it. I was trying to help you think through all these things to see if it's the best move."

"You don't think I can, do you? You think I'm going to flake out and be a colossal failure, just like always. And you'll all sit back and laugh at me, won't you? I'll be the punch line at every family gathering for the rest of time. Michele and her harebrained idea to move to London with some bisexual guy who becomes this great success while she fails. Yet again." I know I'm being irrational, but I'm on a tear here. And maybe, *just maybe,* these are my own self-doubts rearing their ugly head.

Lincoln's on his feet. "It's not that I don't think you can go. It's that I don't want you to go."

Before I can even say 'huh,' Lincoln's closed the distance between us, is cupping my face with his hand, and then his lips are on mine. Soft at first, but as soon as my lips part, the kiss becomes hungry and needy.

"You're not going. You're not going to him. You're going to stay with me."

That gives me pause. No one tells me what to do.

"No one tells me what to do."

He pulls back slightly, my face still in his hand. His other hand is around my waist so I can't go too far. I can't stop looking into his blue eyes, which are searching mine. "I'm telling you I don't want you to go. You should stay here with me."

"You?"

He pulls back fully and is now pacing the room. He won't look at me. "Yes, me," he finally says quietly.

"But you're ... Lincoln. You're like my cousin or something."

"Did that feel like you were kissing your cousin?"

"I've never tried that because, well, yuck." But no, it certainly did *not* feel like I was kissing my cousin. Not even close.

He turns and is back in front of me. "Then stay. Give me a chance. You have people here who will help you get your feet on the ground and become a success. Because we all believe in you. You just need to believe in you too. But, stay for me. Don't go to him. Stay with me."

Chapter 36

The last thing I need is a sleepless night, but that's what I get. How can Lincoln do this to me? It's Lincoln for Pete's sake. He's like my cousin. Except he's not.

Not at all.

After that not-as-awkward-as-I'd-thought-it-would-be kiss, Tony came in. Perfect timing. Or not so perfect. We ate our pizza in relative silence, and then I ran to Tony's room, feigning exhaustion, to avoid even meeting Lincoln's eyes. Not really feigning, since I've had so many ups and downs today that I am really wiped out.

But now there's no way I can sleep.

Lincoln.

Asher.

London.

New York.

Too much in my brain.

I need help.

I pull out my phone and text Christine. Never mind that it's the middle of the night. If she doesn't answer, she doesn't answer. She's the responsible type who puts her phone on silent every night. I need to be more responsible.

I'm surprised that she does text back.

We go back and forth for over an hour. Talking would be easier, but Lincoln's in the next room and I don't want him to hear me talking about him.

I mean, it's Lincoln. *Lincoln.* I've never thought about him that way, not really. Of course, after that kiss, I can think about little else. Dang, he's hot now. He's really not that much younger than I am. In fact, we're closer in age than I am to any of my siblings. Or even to Asher, I'd bet.

And what about Asher?

Oh cripes, I'm all sorts of confused. My brain is such a tangled web that I don't think I'll ever be able to straighten it out.

The morning light dawns through the window and I don't know that I've had more than an hour of sleep combined. My eyes are so puffy that it doesn't look like I've even gotten that much. Awesome. Lincoln's gonna take one look at me and rescind his offer.

Problem solved.

I stumble out to find some nectar of the gods, otherwise known as coffee, and hope there's no one in the kitchen.

My luck must have run out with the winning of the show. Tony, Lincoln, AND Slick Rick are there.

"Looking good this morning." Tony's voice drips with sarcasm.

I give him the appropriate Italian hand gesture and do my best to ignore the other two.

"Did you sleep at all?" At least Lincoln has some concern in his voice. He also has a monopoly on the coffee pot, so I guess I have to interact with him.

I shrug. "Not really."

Slick Rick, not to be ignored, chimes in. "Why not? Thinking about all your pretty dresses and how you're going to spend your prize money?" I wish he would disappear. When did he get back anyway? I sort of hate him. He and Fink totally would make a good couple.

"No, that's not what kept me up." I glance quickly at Lincoln, but can't hold his gaze. Gosh, those eyes are intense. And sexy. Definitely sexy intense.

How did I never see this before?

But it's Lincoln.

It's Lincoln.

Lincoln who lives next door to my aunt and uncle and is virtually a part of the family. Lincoln with the sensitivity that comes from growing up with six sisters. Lincoln who understands my crazy, big, obtrusive family and isn't scared by it. Lincoln who steps up and is there, without even being asked. Lincoln who is smart, Ivy League educated. Lincoln who has been there for me when I needed him. Lincoln who wants nothing more that to see me succeed, and wants to help me do it. Lincoln who has grown up into a fine specimen of a man. Lincoln, who waaaaaay down the road, will make a great husband and father and partner.

Dang.

Lincoln.

Lincoln.

Without care or concern for my appearance, possible morning breath, or the presence of the other two lugs in the room, I put down the coffee cup that Lincoln's just handed me and take his face in my hands.

"Yes," is all I say before I claim his lips with mine.

Somewhere in the deep recesses of my mind, I process the whooping, cat calls, and retching noises Slick Rick and Tony are making. But they don't matter. All that matters is Lincoln.

Well, it does sort of matter that they're in the room, because otherwise I would have wrapped my legs around his waist and let him carry me off to bed. At least I have enough functioning brain cells not to do that.

Not yet, but it is so happening.

"Yes?" Lincoln pulls back just enough to look at me.

"Yes. I know I'm being impulsive again, but that's who I am. And that's why you are good for me. You're not. You think things through. You're, like, rational."

"Thanks, I think?"

"No, it's good. You were right. I need plans, and Lord knows I can't make them on my own. Here is where I have people who can help. Christine is like, literally, a planner. And with Lynn's background in graphic design, if she's not too busy with the baby. And you, and well, everyone. This is where my people are. Moving half a world away with a guy I barely know is not what's best for me. I need to be close to my family. Well, sort of close. I think I could be about three hours away."

A slow, sexy grin spreads over Lincoln's face. It makes my stomach—and somewhere else—flutter. "You know, New York City is about three hours from home."

I match his smile. "I know." I wiggle my eyebrows at him a bit. "It probably seems like a good place to settle, especially with my parents downsizing and all. And there are direct flights from New York to Montabago, so travel won't be so hard. The show pays for my travel anyway, so they can fly me over as much or as little as I need to."

His eyes narrow. "Now, that sounds like you're making some good plans."

I play with the buttons on his shirt. "Well, we all know that I'm not that good at making plans. I'm more of the ideas guy. So, if I surround myself with people who are good at planning and focus, then I should be fine, right?"

"I think you're going to be more than fine."

"I think so too."

****

"I don't think Aunt Maria would approve of this activity." We're lounging in Lincoln's bed after, well, you know.

"I think you shouldn't mention Mama Maria if you want to do that again. No offense, but it's not the visual I want in my head right now, if you know what I mean." Lincoln leans over and brushes my hair off my face. I can only imagine what I look like. Not that he seems to mind.

"I know what you mean." Oh God, that smile.

And, in case you were wondering, he looks even sexier with bed head.

Sigh.

He's quiet for a minute. I'm pretty tired and feel myself start to drift off.

"Are you sure about this?"

I want to make a smart alec comment, but I'm too tired. "I am. I mean, as sure as I ever am about things in life. Although I'm not the best judge sometimes."

"I mean, um, about me ... and not him."

"See previous comment about not being the best judge. He's a prime example. We don't have the same values in life. I have a strong feeling that things would not have worked out so great."

"Have you told him yet?"

"Did you see me call him from the time we were in the kitchen?" I, like my cousin, am fluent in sarcasm.

"What are you going to tell him?"

I think for a minute. "The truth. That in the long run, he and I are probably not that compatible. And that I need someone who complements me, not competes with me. And frankly, that I'm almost positive you were made for me."

Epilogue

She's now officially Princess Maryn of the United Republic of Montabago. And she looks even more stunning that I ever thought possible. I can't stop crying. Which is odd, because I'm one of the only ones here moved to tears. I hope the audience at home is crying. That dress is gorgeous, and she's radiant. I deserve some tears.

Stupid stoic royals. I'm so glad I'm not one of them.

Two weeks in the palace has been quite enough for me. Although, maybe it's the two weeks separation from Lincoln that made it feel too long. I could have had him flown over here as my official guest, but I thought it was only fair to bring Kira. The wedding party, not to mention the bride, would be naked, if it weren't for her.

She's crying even harder than I am.

"I know, right? She looks beautiful."

Kira starts crying even more. "Stan left me."

She's been here for four days, and hasn't said anything up until this point. "What?"

"When I got home, after the final taping, he was gone. He'd left Fleur with my mom and took off."

"Oh my gosh, Kira, why didn't you say

something?" Trying to whisper when there's news of this magnitude is difficult. But we're still in church and the ceremony is still going on.

"Well, you were all so happy, and there was so much work to do. I'm trying not to think about it."

Kira's right. I'm a crappy friend. She didn't have to help me—she could have done touristy things here, but she gave up her free time to assist me with last minute alterations. And all I did was talk about Lincoln—non-stop.

Our tears pick up a bit, this time for a bride left alone rather than the beaming bride before us. The organ music swells and the newly married couple turns to face the full cathedral for the first time as husband and wife.

"Dang, Vanilla, I know I've told you before, but you did an incredible job. You deserved to win."

I blush at the compliment but secretly feel the same way. I try to picture this day with Fink or Asher's looks, but can't.

Asher.

Yeah, that's a bridge that may have been burnt.

He was not happy when I told him that I wouldn't be moving to London with him. Turns out, he's a bit of an opportunist. He was hoping to convince me to go into business with him, as a junior partner, to capitalize on my momentum from the show. He didn't say it in so many words, but I gleaned as much from one of his tirades. I don't even know if he realizes that that's what he intended on doing. I'm almost positive that he didn't purposefully set out to use me. It's sort of who he is, I think. I'm trying hard not to be mad at him. Trying.

Thank goodness Lincoln had the wherewithal to talk some sense into me. And that he spoke up when he did. I can't believe I didn't see him right in front of me all this time. Like he was part of the whole big picture, but I never noticed that detail.

Kira wipes her eyes. "Okay, enough of that. Good riddance to bad rubbish and all that crap."

We're filing out of the cathedral. I can't wait to see the reception. I mean, it's a *royal* reception. Nothing's ever going to top this. The event planners worked closely with me on my vision to go along with the attendants' wardrobe. The florist nailed the flowers, except maybe they're even better than I'd ever imagined. I have to do an interview when I first get to the reception. After that, I'm getting Kira good and drunk, and we're going to find her a nice wedding guest to shack up with and forget her louse soon-to-be-ex-husband.

For the church we're dressed in conservative day dresses, but the reception is black tie. We've got about three hours to change and get restyled. Kira's quiet again and doesn't want to talk. "I'm going to take a nap before the reception," she says, excusing herself to her room.

I take off my dress, a New Michele original of course. It's a 50s era fitted dress that looks like a full skirt from the back, while having a narrow front. Sort of like a pencil skirt and a poodle skirt had a baby. It's got a conservative boat neck, three-quarter sleeves, and a nice deep V in the back. There are, of course, buttons marching down the narrow part of the skirt in the front. Sounds weird, but I love the way it came out. I actually have a store-bought gown for the reception. I didn't have time to make my own, and the show financed the wardrobe anyway.

I should probably nap too, but I'm too keyed up. I open my laptop to see if Lincoln's available for a video chat. I've been working on a website and catalogue, and researching studio space and warehouse facilities in the city. If the people contacting my Etsy site are any indication, I'm going to be quite busy. I won't be able to handle all the sewing on my own. I'm going to have to hire people to make my clothes.

That thought blows me away. This is all sort of surreal.

Lincoln's face pops up on my screen. "Hey beautiful, how was the wedding?"

"Oh, it was great. She looked so good. Kira and I were sobbing like babies, but we were the only ones. These royals don't let anything show."

"So, not at all like your family."

That makes me laugh. "Not quite."

There's a lot of movement on his end of the screen. "What are you doing? You're bouncing all over the place."

"Oh, I'm walking."

"What do you have on the agenda for today? Are you heading into work?" I'm about eight hours ahead of Lincoln, so that seems about right. Maybe he's even a little late.

"I'm on special assignment with the company today. On location."

"Oh, that's cool. Anything exciting?"

"Not sure yet, but it seems promising."

We're interrupted by a knock on the door. "Hang

on, there's someone at the door. I hope there's not a wardrobe malfunction."

"That would be terrible."

I hurry over to the door of the suite where the knocking has continued. Yes, Kira and I have a suite in the palace. Wow, I just like the way that sounds.

"Hello?" I say, pulling the door open.

"I certainly hope there are no wardrobe malfunctions tonight. I'd hate for someone's breasts to be exposed." Lincoln's grinning, phone still in his hand.

SQUEEEEEEEEE!

"Can you please tell the network that I'm being harassed by one of their minions? Also, I have a boyfriend, and I don't think he'd appreciate that very much."

"Actually, your boyfriend would appreciate seeing your breasts very much right about now."

I pull him in and give him the most welcoming kiss I can. "I only have a few minutes before I have to get ready, but I'll see what I can do."

Lincoln follows me into the room, letting out a low whistle. "Wow, nice digs."

"Yeah, I've got an in with the princess. But that's neither here nor there. What are you doing here?"

"I have an in with the studio. Plus, it's not like I'm going to miss my girlfriend's biggest night."

"Say that again."

"Biggest night?"

"No, girlfriend."

"Oh, that my *girlfriend* is the most beautiful, insanely talented fashion designer, and after tonight is going to be known worldwide."

"Yeah, that's about it."

He kisses me again. "Plus, I missed you."

I give him a quick kiss on the nose. "Sap."

"And proud of it."

He grabs me and pulls me close again. I lead him to my room where I'm able to give him a proper welcome.

After, I look at him. "I'm going to be in trouble. Now I have to get the royal hairdresser here to fix my hair. You made a mess of it."

"Turn around. Let me."

Lincoln's quickly moving bobby pins, and I can feel my hair being twisted and gently pulled. "Done."

I look in the mirror, and by George, he's fixed my hair. It doesn't look the same as it did, but it'll work for the rest of the night.

"But how?"

"Six sisters, the only boy. It was a lonely existence on the days Tony wasn't around."

I look from side to side, checking it out from all angles. Unbelievable. "Is there anything you can't do?"

He smiles, that sexy smile that makes me weak in the knees. "I don't think so."

I head over to the wardrobe, pull on my foundation garments, and slide my gown over my head. "We've got a royal couple to go celebrate."

"Oh, that's right. I thought this was all about you."

"Ha, I wish. We're celebrating the start of a beautiful romance."

"Them or us?" Lincoln's buttoning up his shirt. How did I not notice he was in a tuxedo when we were video chatting?

"Us, because I know, I've found my Prince Charming."

"And you know what that means."

I smile and nod. I am so ready for my happily ever after.

The End

Acknowledgments

My beta readers: Becky Monson, Wendy Nagel, Michele Vagianelis, Tracy Krimmer, Cahren Morris, and Mary Rose Kopach—thank you for all your amazing feedback and support.

Becky I say this every time, but this cover is my favorite. For reals this time.

Becky and Wendy, thank you for all your encouragement and for telling me I'm funny. I mean, I know I'm funny but the rest of the world (namely my husband) doesn't always share that viewpoint.

Thank you to Melissa Baldwin for making me report numbers. We are so doing this tandem writing thing again.

Thank you Karen Pirozzi for being my editor extraordinaire. Sorry about my poor timing. I wish we could be on perpetual summer vacation. And to Marlene Engel, for your eagle eye.

My writing groups continue to get me through. Thanks especially to my Albany NaNoWriMo group. This book is a product of the April and July camps, so sign up!

I have to thank my grandmother, Genevieve Kopach, for passing on her love of not only sewing but writing. In the hours spent at my machine and computer, I feel your influence.

As always, without my family—Mom, Dad, Patrick, Jake, and Sophia—I'd be no where. Thank you for your patience, your understanding, and your inspiration. You know what story I mean, Jake and Sophia.

About the Author

Telling stories of resilient women, Kathryn Biel hails from upstate New York and is a wife and mother to two wonderful and energetic kids. In between being Chief Home Officer and Director of Child Development of the Biel household, she works as a school-based physical therapist. She attended Boston University and received her Doctorate in Physical Therapy from The Sage Colleges. After years of writing countless letters of medical necessity for wheelchairs, finding increasingly creative ways to encourage the government and insurance companies to fund her clients' needs, and writing entertaining annual Christmas letters, she decided to take a shot at writing the kind of novel that she likes to read. Her musings and rants can be found on her personal blog, Biel Blather. She is the author of *Good Intentions* (2013), *Hold Her Down* (2014), *I'm Still Here* (2014), *Jump, Jive, and Wail* (2015), *Killing Me Softly* (2015), and *Completions and Connections: A Romantic Holiday Novella* (2015), and *Live for This* (2016).

If you've enjoyed this book, please help the author out by leaving a review on Amazon and Goodreads. A few minutes of your time makes a huge difference to an indie author!

Made in the USA
Middletown, DE
17 June 2019